OTHER BOO
*The* ~
Kee~
Mak~
Riding Rebel
Kola
A Very Essien Christmas
Freddie Entangled
Freddie Untangled

*Bound Series*
Bound to Fate
Bound to Ransom
Bound to Passion
Bound to Favor
Bound to Liberty

*The Challenge Series*
Valentine
Engaged
Worthy
Captive

*The Ben & Selina Trilogy*
Scars
Secrets
Scores

*Men of Valor Series*
His Treasure
His Strength
His Princess

*Enders Series*
Duke: Prince of Hearts
Xandra: Killer of Kings
Osagie: Bad Santa
Rough Diamond
Tough Alliance

*Royal House of Saene Series*
His Captive Princess
The Tainted Prince
The Future King
Saving Her Guard
Screwdriver

*Others*
Haunted
Outcast
Sacrifice
Black Soul
Scar's Redemption

# AGAINST THE RUN OF PLAY

## VIVA CITY FC BOOK TWO

## KIRU TAYE

First Published in Great Britain in 2024 by
LOVE AFRICA PRESS
103 Reaver House, 12 East Street, Epsom KT17 1HX
www.loveafricapress.com

LOVE
AFRICA
PRESS

Home of African Love Stories

# Viva City FC Season 1 Books:

Game of Two Halves by Unoma Nwankwor
Against the Run of Play by Kiru Taye

# AGAINST THE
# RUN OF PLAY

VIVA CITY FC BOOK TWO

KIRU TAYE

# Blurb

Soccer player and reformed bad boy, Asher Uzodimma, is struggling through a challenging season. Due to a string of injuries, he finds himself relegated to the bench during crucial games as his team battles for promotion into the league's top division. Frustrated, he falls back on some old habits and escapes to find solace where he encounters the vibrant Vivi. Yet, spending only two days with her brings a sense of calm and stability back into his life. She possesses all the qualities he never realised he desired in a woman, and his yearning to be in her presence grows stronger with each passing day. Nevertheless, when he finally learns her full identity, she quickly becomes the last woman anyone wants for him.

Vivacious and fun-loving Vivi Osondu is currently in seclusion after the highly publicised end to her turbulent relationship. She needs a break to reevaluate her life and dedicate time to self-reflection. Meeting Asher brings back her laughter, which had been missing for months, and each time she lays eyes on him, her stomach fills with a delightful sense of excitement. However, he's part of the famous crowd, and she's made a conscious decision to steer clear of that world, so she chooses to walk away. But Asher is determined to turn the game around both on and off the pitch, against the run of play.

# Playlist

War by ArrDee ft Aitch

Beautiful Disaster by Matteo Bocelli

Waiting in Vain by Bob Marley & The Wailers

Blinded by your Grace by Stormzy ft MNEK

Playing Games by Summer Walker ft Bryson
Tiller

Every Praise by Hezekiah Walker

Hide & Seek Stormzy

Something Real by Summer Walker

Essence by Wizkid ft Tems

Location by Dave ft Burna Boy

Big God by Tim Godfrey ft Moses Bliss

Listen on Spotify:
https://open.spotify.com/playlist/4Plj71aMRJSQ
Dhuz9h3xwF

# Fuchsia

The colour fuchsia is bright and bold. Its energy is instantly uplifting. Fuchsia colour is considered fun and youthful, but not naïve. The colour fuchsia evokes the same boldness that it brings, too, meaning that fuchsia can inspire confident and assertive behaviour. ~ Adobe.com

In art and fashion, fuchsia is its own colour that evokes romance, excitement, happiness, and achievement. The colour fuchsia is more vibrant than pink but warmer than purple. ~ Creative booster

## Vivi

"Here they come!"

A thunderous cheer goes up in the stadium as the football players run out of the tunnel onto the field.

A bolt of excitement shoots down my spine. My heart races with every breath of the chilly winter air I inhale, and I clap along with the other spectators in the packed 25,000-seater stadium.

Even when the crowd calms somewhat, my foot keeps bouncing erratically against the concrete terrace floor.

My cousin and bestie, Temi, leans across the seat and shouts in my ear. "Vivi, you have to calm down. You're vibrating like a jumping bean. Anyone would think your man is playing in the World Cup final."

Her teasing words snap me out of my daze. Tilting my head, I catch the cheeky smile on her face. She's pulling my leg, of course. And I nudge her ribs with my elbow in playful retaliation, making her giggle as she sits back.

She's not half wrong. It wasn't the soccer World Cup final, but around these parts, it might as well be. Oh, and around these parts, we call it football, just so you know.

"It's a big game for Owen. For DPR. A derby," I reply, shrugging with nonchalance I don't exactly feel. "The nerves are natural."

Owen Price is *my man* and the top scorer at Duke's Park Rangers football club, or DPR, a team in the EFL Championship. We're currently in the stadium at Chapel Road for the home match against Viva City Panthers.

I should spit when I say that club's name. Around here, DPR supporters call them Viva City

Panta*loons*, emphasis on the 'loons,' and they in turn refer to DPR as 'Derangers.'

These two clubs have a rivalry going back to way before I was born, back to when the clubs were formed in the early 20th century. It doesn't help how the stadiums are located less than four miles from each other. Back in the day, you couldn't walk into any pub in the area with the wrong colours and not get your butt kicked.

So, it isn't just any old derby.

You've heard of the Manchester Derby: Man City vs Man U?

The North London rivalry between Arsenal and Tottenham Hotspur?

Or even the Merseyside competitiveness of Liverpool FC vs Everton FC.

Well, let me introduce you to the Viva City Derby. A clash of arch-rivals.

Duke's Park Rangers vs Viva City Panthers. DPR vs VCP, for short.

This is one of the biggest games in the season. Not only because of their historic rivalry—both teams are in the top-half of the EFL Championship table and vying for promotion spots into the Premier League.

"But it's more than that, though, isn't it, Vi?" Temi comments, shortening my name like she does sometimes. "You're thinking about later. About—"

"Shhhh. Don't say it…" I interrupt her.

"Don't jinx it," she completes one of our favourite sayings.

One thing about football or sports fans in general, we have rituals and superstitions. For example, if we did a certain thing or wore a certain attire on the day our team wins after a run of losses, we repeat those activities and wear the same clothes on future match days hoping the universe will recognise our contributions and allow our team to continue winning.

Might sound illogical, but have you met sport fans?

Anyway, the point is, we try not to do anything to jeopardise our team's success. And we tend to apply the same rationality to other aspects of our lives.

Hence my reluctance to talk or even think about the surprise I've planned for later in case it's ruined. Needless to say, it's huge and could change my future.

So instead, I say nothing and shake out my shoulders and smooth my palms over the sleek tresses of my lace-front wig. Owen likes my hair sleek smooth, but the constant heat involved in styling my natural hair was damaging it. So, this is my compromise. And it gives my hair a much-needed rest from the dreaded, unpredictable British weather.

"See, eh? Don't worry about it. You've got this," she continues, grabbing my hand and giving it a warm squeeze.

"I hope so." The butterflies remain in my tummy, but her reassurance calms my nerves a little.

I tug my coat tighter around my dress. It's freezing tonight, and I'm in a black midi bodycon dress and matching lace-up wedge ankle boots. Owen asked me to wear it tonight. It's the outfit I wore the night we met. He says I'm his good luck charm.

Remember what I said about soccer superstitions? Well, this girl will do what it takes for her man to win the Viva City derby.

Temi wears jeans and the club jersey under her coat and scarf. Her hair is in long braids, tumbling over her shoulders and back. A heart-shaped face with high cheekbones and bowed lips. She wears her confidence in the tilt of her jaw and warm, sparkling eyes.

When we were younger, people mistook us for sisters. Understandable, since our mothers are siblings. We're children of immigrant parents growing up in the United Kingdom but immersed in the Nigerian culture at home. We became closer as we got older, and we don't let anything come between us.

We've been through so much, sharing experiences, music festivals, and holidays abroad. Temi's father is a keen fan and supports Duke's Park Rangers, which is how we became supporters, too.

So, when I met Owen Price, local boy and DPR's star striker at a party and we started dating, my family blessed our relationship. Eighteen months on, and I'm ready for the next step. Hence the reason for my jittery nerves.

However, the loud spectators, roving cameras, and chirpy commentators remind me of my surroundings.

The big screen flashes pictures of the opposition players, and one catches my attention.

Asher Uzodimma. No 11. Lean, powerful body, chiselled face, and walnut-brown skin. Best attacking winger on the team if not the entire EFL Championship league. I enjoy watching post-match interviews with him. There's always a vulnerability about him that belies his strength on camera. Sometimes, I wish Owen had similar qualities.

Not that I would ever say this aloud to my man.

Because Owen has a running rivalry between him and Asher. And he voices his bitterness at every opportunity. The two men seem to always want to get the better of each other. Even the media seems fixated on their competitive behaviours.

Today will be no different.

Both handsome men of the same height. They are both powerful athletes and on paper evenly matched.

However, whenever the two of them clash in the derby games, Asher always seems to have the upper hand. This only aggravates Owen more.

Let today's match be different, I pray silently. I need Owen in a good mood later.

*****

A fiasco is one way to describe tonight's game.

I asked the universe for a different outcome to the usual run of play between the two football rivals, and it delivered.

Just not in the way I expected or wanted. Not at all.

Someone up there is having a laugh at my expense. Because '*Warris dis, biko,*' as my Igbo mother would say when she puts on her Nigerian accent. This shit would be funny if it weren't such a disaster.

I suppose I should have been more specific about how different I wanted the game. Ironic, really. Still, it was definitely not like the previous clashes.

For one, Owen received two yellow cards, a subsequent red card, and was sent off during the match. This means a three-match suspension. First time it happened since we started dating. Not sure about his entire football career. He's received bookings before, but never a red card. Not to my knowledge, anyway.

And guess who he fouled.

Asher Uzodimma.

I don't even know what happened. Our team was ahead by two goals to one after halftime. There was a free kick. Owen and Asher collided in a tackle. Then Asher crumpled to the ground, holding his leg.

At the time, I even joined in booing him because I thought he was playing up just to get Owen booked. But the medical staff ran onto the field. Next, the referee used the VAR to review the incident and called Owen to the spot, issuing him a yellow card followed by a red card.

The medical team stretchered Asher off the field and his team's coach made a substitution.

Meanwhile, DPR played on with ten men. Without Owen.

So, we went from being two-one up to drawing two-all at the final whistle. Instead of earning three points and going to the top of the league table, we ended up with a meagre one point and stuck behind the leaders.

*Grrrrr.* I could scream.

Still, it could have been worse. We could've lost.

I shudder at the thought. I have to keep it together for my man's sake.

Okay, the tackle might have been a little excessive.

But it was a derby. Tempers always frayed a little. It was part of the game.

Although it seems Owen's temper hasn't mellowed even now because he's driving down the dual carriageway like a demon racer in a Porsche. He's been in a foul mood since.

Reaching out, I turn down the knob on the radio blasting 'War' by ArrDee and Aitch. The track is one he plays on a loop to psych himself up for match days. But the match is over, so he needs to calm down.

"Babe, slow down." My voice is soft to soothe him as I place my palm on his arm.

The last thing he needs is to get a speeding ticket, or worse. Plus, we have to get to his apartment in one piece so I can unleash my surprise.

He doesn't respond immediately, and I think he'll ignore me. Eventually, his foot eases off the pedal, and the car slows towards the designated speed limit.

I exhale in relief when we take the exit towards the gated complex where he lives. It's not a mansion like you'd expect for players in the Premier League. But it's still more than most can afford.

My phone beeps, and I lift it to check the message. It's from Temi.

**Where are you guys?**

*Almost there*, I type and send. *We're just approaching Carter Close.*

**Great**, she replies. After the match, she went ahead to ensure everything is set up properly. She is my wing woman.

Another glance at Owen's pensive face makes my tummy clench, and I type quickly.

*Maybe I should cancel everything. Owen is not in a good mood.*

The superstitious part of me screams that the outcome of today's football match is an omen of things to come.

Another message pings with Temi's reply.

**That's expected. But his mood will improve when he walks in here. You've been planning this for a while. Don't bottle it.**

Another heavy breath escapes me and I send: *Fine.*

She has a point. Sure, I can leave Owen to wallow in the annoying outcome of the match. Or I can follow through with the event which will lift his spirits and celebrate our relationship.

When Owen pulls into his allocated parking, I don't wait for him to come around. He won't in his current mood. I hustle out and follow him into the building. It is an old manor converted into apartments about eight years ago. He bought his off-plan when he became a first team player at DPR.

He is in his two-piece, light-grey V-neck long-sleeve pullover sweatshirt and drawstring tapered joggers and matching trainers. Bling around his neck and wrist. All high-end brands. My man loves the good things in life, and so do I.

He walks with clipped and fast footsteps. I'm in the high-heeled boots. I hurry to keep up with him as he enters the foyer and heads towards the stairs. There's a lift, but with only three levels, we can walk.

"Babe, hold up," I call out. I don't want him getting upstairs without me.

He pauses with one foot on the first rung. When I overtake him and place his hand on my hip, he exhales a sigh and follows me up, his arm around me. It's the first time he's held me tonight, and I can't resist the smile playing on my lips.

My man loves my buttocks, and I know he won't resist once I flash them at him. He couldn't resist me the first time he saw me in this dress, and it works like a treat whenever I wear it.

By the time we reach his apartment, he's feeling me up. He pushes me against the door, proceeds to kiss me, and tries to tug my dress up.

"Owen, stop. Not yet." I pull away.

He lifts his head, looking confused and annoyed. Then he shakes his head and inserts the key into the lock. The door pops open, and he steps in, reaching to the wall to flick on the switch.

An orange glow fills his luxurious apartment foyer as I follow him inside. The walls are cream, and the floor tiles shine from the polish. The potted plant I gifted him is in the corner, adding a splash of colour to the otherwise minimalist space.

He enters the living room, and there's an eruption of "Surprise!" which makes him gasp, eyes wide, hand on his chest.

In his sitting room are Temi and Dave, Owen's friend, who is also my co-host on my podcast, *Loud and Proud*. Their eyes shine with anticipation, and their lips curl in supportive smiles.

I recruited the two of them to orchestrate this surprise. They transformed the apartment into a realm of enchantment. Twinkling fairy lights are strung across the ceiling, casting a warm glow over the room while delicate rose petals lead to a circle of candles in the centre. Tripods and cameras are placed strategically to record everything, one to livestream, the other for editing later.

Temi set the dining area up with culinary delights she prepared, an array of delectable treats. The aromas mingle with the scent of flowers decorating the room. Soft RnB music— Summer Walker's 'Something Real'—plays from the speakers. I meticulously planned every detail.

"What's going on? What are you doing here?" Owen's gaze bounces from the other two in the room to me.

I take a deep breath, my heart aflutter with renewed nerves and excitement. Temi gives me an encouraging nod, her presence a pillar of strength.

"I'll explain," I say as I step forward, hands trembling as Temi hands me the small velvet box. The room falls silent, all eyes on me. It's Valentine's Day in a Leap year. I'll leave you to guess the rest.

I lower onto my knees. The floor is hard and cold, but I ignore the discomfort and reach for my man's hand.

"What are you doing?" he asks in a harsh whisper, his expression twisted with an expression I can't decipher.

"If you let me get a word in, I'll tell you," I whisper with a smile, conscious he's not exactly reacting the way I predicted.

"No!" He withdraws from me, and I sway, bracing my hand on the floor so I don't face-plant on it. "No. I'm not letting you do it."

A coldness hits my core, and a sickness curdles my stomach. My throat constricts. "What are you saying?"

He swivels in my direction, his face twisted in disgust. "I'm saying that whatever you think you're doing here is not working." He stomps towards the door. "Actually, by the time I get back, I want you gone."

"Owen!" I call out, but he's left the flat. The slamming door rattles my bones, and I slump on the floor, a little too dazed to rise.

Movement catches the corner of my eye, reminding me I'm not alone. Temi slashes her rigid horizontal hand through the air in a 'cut' sign to Dave while she hurries to my side. He picks up the mounted recording devices and disconnects them.

Oh, no! Not only did Dave and Temi witness the disaster of a proposal, but an army of followers saw it, too.

Nausea rolls through me as Temi settles beside me and gives me a hug. Tears gather and fall, my chest a ball of desolate emotions.

All I can whisper is, "What the hell just happened?"

# 2

## Asher

There's always something special about travelling to Africa.

My career as a professional footballer has taken me to the four corners of the globe. Yet, each visit to this continent feels like a homecoming.

Before the private airplane touches down at the international airport in Zanzibar and we disembark, my senses heighten with anticipation, battling with the feeling of dread weighting my chest.

Yes, I'm conflicted about this trip. Still, I push aside my worries as my travelling companions and I fast-track through customs and immigrations. My friends, Zafe Essien and Mak Phillips, and I have flown over four thousand miles to be here.

We're attending the destination birthday event for the 'king of finance' tycoon Chief Aloysius Essien, who also is Zafe's adopted father and my uncle in-law. My big cousin Ebony Duru is married to Zafe's oldest brother, Felix. My mother's maiden name is Duru. So, they are family to me.

A private hire SUV is waiting for us. We load our baggage into the boot before climbing into the vehicle. I sit in front with the friendly chauffeur while my friends take the back seats. Then the driver begins the last leg of our journey to the holiday resort, where we'll spend the long weekend.

I watch the scenery whizzing past the window, and a smile tugs at my lips. The sun is bright in the clear, blue sky, just as the people I've met so far are warm and welcoming. The paved roads are lined with leafy green trees and widely spaced, low-rise pastel-coloured buildings. The tallest I see is only three storeys high. A far cry from the gloomy, rainy concrete jungle I left behind.

*Should I be here?*

The thought is a worm eating into my mind as a hollowness sits in my chest like a heavy load.

Zafe and Mak chatter away during the journey in excitement, but I barely say anything, only responding in monosyllables. When they ask if I'm okay, I deflect and make an excuse about being tired from the flight.

I flew from London to Milan to join them on the private jet for the journey to this island resort. Therefore, I covered more aerial distance. They seem to buy my excuse and leave me to my musings.

I should be excited about spending the weekend with family and friends. Enthusiastic about partying. At any other time previously, I would have been the one planning out all the fun.

But my life changed drastically about a month ago.

I play professional football in the Championship, the penultimate club competition in the English Football League or EFL for short. My team, Viva City Panthers FC, is fighting to top the table and win a coveted promotion spot into the EFL Premier League.

However, four weeks ago, I sustained an injury that could have cost me my football career.

All because of a horrible tackle by a player from the opposing team during a match.

I don't even want to think about the culprit. I've given Owen effing Price enough room in my head, which has only fuelled my bitterness.

My fingers clench around the armrest beside me.

Thinking about the man sets my teeth on edge.

Yes, I'm bitter because he gets to continue playing football while I'm signed off for the next God-knows-how long!

Sure, he was sent off from the match, suspended for three games, and fined. But he's returned and has been featured in the team line-up since the incident. While I must endure pain and therapy and a long period of absence from playing the game I love.

Talk about FOMO. That's me right now.

My team played a crucial game today, but I wasn't there. For the first time since I became a professional player, I've missed four weeks of playing mid-season. And I will miss more to come.

In my weak moments, when depression creeps over me, I feel frustrated and helpless.

Because it could get so much worse. If I don't play this season, I could lose the chance to do the one thing I've worked hard for all my playing life—to play football in the Premier League. If VCP doesn't make the promotion spots.

The driver pulls up outside the hotel reception about ninety minutes after we departed from the airport. The resort is in the north-west corner of the island. As I step out of the vehicle, the sound of sea washing over sand reaches me in a regular, gentle cadence. The concierge greets us, and the service staff wheel our luggage into the foyer for checking in. The process doesn't take long once our IDs are confirmed.

Our accommodation is in an exclusive, secluded section of the five-star beach resort reserved for the Essien family and their invited guests. We and our luggage are loaded onto electric buggies and driven along a tree-lined sandy lane with the ocean waves lapping the beach only metres away.

The breeze is refreshing, and the view is amazing. We go past single-level buildings with thatched roofs and surrounded by flowering shrubs and palm trees. The ocean blue, white sand, emerald shrubs—yes, amazing doesn't seem enough to describe the exquisiteness.

"This place is beautiful," Zafe calls out from the lead buggy.

We're on three different buggies, with a driver each and the baggage in the back racks. The vehicles slow down and stop.

Two young women step onto the stone-paved street outside a wooden building on stilts with a thatched roof.

"Wow! Is that Ranti?" Mak comments in awe.

I recognise the women, Inna and Ranti. Inna is Zafe's younger sister, and Ranti is their cousin. They must have been here a few days because they appear relaxed in their casual attires, unlike us, who've only just arrived.

"Zafe!" Inna exclaims and runs towards us.

We climb out of the buggies and collide in greetings and welcome. However, drama ensues when Mak tries to talk to Ranti, and she storms off. Those two must have history I don't know about.

The staff ushers us into our shared accommodation, a bungalow. Mak and I share a room while Zafe shares with his younger cousin Yomi, who is also Ranti's twenty-one-year-old brother. There is a living space with sofas, television, and a kitchenette with a coffeemaker, fridge-freezer, and other mod-cons.

"So, Mak. How are you? How is Milan?" Inna asks as we carry our bags in.

This is the part of the reunion I dread. When someone who genuinely cares about me asks me a question about my wellbeing, do I lie or tell them the crushing truth?

These people hold high expectations of me. They know how hard I worked to get where I am. So how can I possibly tell them I'm afraid and despairing sometimes?

I'm almost twenty-nine years old and most footballers retire by age thirty-four. At best I have another year or two of playing at my peak before my body starts declining after I hit thirty. Biology dictates it. This season is the best chance for my team to progress into the Premier League. But we're not doing too well at the moment and I can't influence the results because I'm out injured. If we miss out on this opportunity, my dream of playing topflight football will disappear.

The heavy hollowness returns to my chest, and my breathing becomes shallow. The need to escape the inevitable questioning grips me, and I hurry down the short corridor into the bedroom I'll be sharing with Mak. I dump my bag and return into the living room, heading towards the exit.

"Asher, where are you going?" Inna calls out.

"I need to go for a walk. I need fresh air to clear my head," I say and keep walking.

"But you said you were tired," Mak says.

"From sitting down for too long."

"Don't forget, the dinner party is tonight."

"I won't. I'll be back with plenty of time to prepare."

They seem satisfied with my responses, and I escape outdoor. Sunset isn't far off, and a cool breeze rustles the leaves. There are low hedges demarcating the buildings and the streets. Between the pure white sands, the turquoise ocean, the golden sun, and the emerald-green foliage, the place appears magical, especially with the buildings designed to blend in.

I head back towards the main resort building. It's a fifteen minutes' walk. I don't mind. I spotted a bar lounge while we were checking in. At the reception, I enquire if the bar shows European soccer. One concierge volunteers to show me the sports bar.

My heart rate increases with excitement. I could stream the matches on my digital devices but it's always better to watch on the big screen if not live. So, it seems there's a silver lining to being here.

You can take the footballer out of the game, but you can't take the game out of the footballer.

Even on an island in the middle of the Indian Ocean, I can't escape it. I don't want to escape it. Football is my career. My life.

"This is the sports bar." The concierge holds the swinging door to the single-level annex on the other side of a swimming pool.

"Thank you," I say and pull notes out of my wallet to give him from the ones I changed at the airport. Then I walk into the lounge.

It has low, dark furniture and a massive flatscreen television mounted on a pillar at the opposite end of the bar counter. It's playing a game from the Premier League, and satisfaction rushes through me. The place is half full of men, mostly white. It seems the bar is for the tourists, not the locals.

I walk to the counter and climb onto a tall stool.

"Good evening, sir. What can I get you?" The man's voice is tinged with a Swahili accent.

"What bottled beer do you have?"

He mentions the choices, and I order the one he recommends because the locals enjoy it.

"Are you a resort guest or a visitor?" he asks.

"Guest." I pull out the little envelope with the keycard. The bungalows have names, not numbers. "Acacia Lodge."

"And your name, sir?" he asks as he enters the details into his point-of-sale system.

"Asher Uzodimma."

His head whips up, and he stares at my face again as his lips curl into a grin. "I thought I recognised you. Welcome, sir."

I glance around to check if he's talking to someone else. But there's no one beside me. I rarely get recognised by random strangers in foreign countries because I don't play top-flight football like Zafe and Mak. The driver who picked us from the airport even recognised them. So, it's a little difficult to accept this man knows me.

"Do you know me?" I ask in astonishment.

"Of course, I recognise the top scorer in the EFL Championship this season. Well, that was before your injury. Your team isn't doing so well in your absence. How are you?"

So shocked and pleased by his kind words, I blurt out without a second thought. "I'm not doing so well. Recovery is long and hard. I want to be out there playing. Not just stuck in physio all the time."

"I can only imagine. I will pray for your speedy recovery, my friend." He nods in understanding and pats my hand.

"Thank you so much. What's your name?"

Chatting with him releases the heavy hollowness in my chest. Perhaps coming to this island is a blessing. Perhaps I need it to combat the aching loneliness I felt for weeks.

"My name is Faraji. Excuse me." He goes off to serve another customer.

Swivelling, I grab my drink and face the screen.

"That's a foul!"

I crane my neck towards the loud female voice and find a Black woman sitting at a table in an alcove beside the counter. She isn't immediately visible when you walk into the lounge, which is why I didn't notice her before.

She's sitting alone with just a glass of her drink on the table along with a mobile phone. Is she by herself? The only other people at the bar are the white men sitting closer to the screen. She's as far away as possible from them in this place.

I look her over and am dumbstruck at how beautiful and carefree she is. She has a dark pink or fuchsia-coloured shirt over a white tank top and a pair of white cotton shorts. The contrast to her dark complexion seems to make her skin luminous even from there.

On her feet are white sandals. Her toenails are painted the same colour as her shirt. Same as her long fingernails. Her natural hair is packed into a puffy afro bun and seems to have a pink streak running through it. She is toned and athletic, yet the curves of her butt fill out the shorts, and her legs stretch for miles under the table. I can only see her side profile, but I bet her face card is amazing.

Her gaze is fixated on the screen, and she is animated. I'm in awe and drawn to the rapt way she engages with the game and her reactions to the action on screen. This is a true soccer fan. There is no way to fake the body expressions.

I have siblings, sisters who occasionally watch the big games like AFCON or the World Cup. Even my exes were never genuine fans of the sports. They mostly loved the player. Not the game. Even when we watched games at home, they would always get distracted by their phones and spend more time on those.

But this woman hasn't once touched her phone since I noticed her. She's gesticulating, mouthing obscenities, making faces. When one of the team scores, she leaps off the chair briefly before settling back.

I spend more time watching her than the game. Even without seeing her face, I want to take my drink and go to her. A woman who looks like her and loves football I want to meet.

But from the position of her table, I'm guessing she's trying to avoid people, maybe because she doesn't want to be disturbed during the game. I don't want to intrude while the match is on. Maybe she'll take a break during half-time, and I can then talk to her briefly.

So, I wait. Ten minutes later, the game goes to half-time. She stands and walks towards the exit marked *Toilets*. When she returns, she sits in the chair and scrolls through her phone. Still, no one approaches her.

"Faraji," I call the bartender who is wiping washed glasses. "I want to buy the lady over there a drink. Please get her whatever she's drinking."

"She drinks Smirnoff Ice." He flips the towel over his shoulder.

"Okay. Add it to my tab."

He nods and grabs the bottle from the fridge before passing me the tab to sign. I scrawl my signature before he takes the drink and walks over to the other side of the lounge, where the woman is sitting.

I don't hear what he says as he places the bottle on her table. At first, she shakes her head and pushes the bottle back towards him. Then he says something else to her.

For the first time, she turns her head and looks in my direction. My heart rate kicks up a notch, and my mouth waters.

Damn. I was right. Her face card is off-the charts. She is peng. Beautiful. Attractive. I don't have the freaking words.

Her eyes widen, narrow, then widen again. It's as if she can't make up her mind, and emotions chase themselves across her face. Mostly disbelief and suspicion, then... Does she recognise me?

I can swear I see a flash of recognition before she turns away and says something to the barman. Does she know who I am? Is it possible that two different people would recognise me halfway across the world?

A part of me—my ego—wants the recognition, wants to feel celebrated like my peers, wants the fans and the adulation. But the problem is that when you stop playing, when you're not on their TVs every week during the season, most people forget about you. I haven't been in a stadium or on a TV screen for a month. That's a lifetime for spectators.

Yet, another part of me wants her to get to know me on a human level. I want her to know me as Asher, not the sports star. It's a well-known fact that many people are attracted to the celebrity, money, and lifestyle associated with a sports athlete. Many of my exes were about that life, and it irks me they seem to love the lifestyle more than they ever loved me.

Faraji returns behind the counter.

"She says thank you," he says to me before continuing with his duties and serving other customers.

Is that all?

I glance at the woman, and her eyes are on her phone. It's like I don't exist to her.

*She's swathed in fuchsia,*
*The beautiful ego crusher,*
*A vision of grace,*
*A smile on her face.*
*Her presence commands the room,*
*But she's got no time for fools.*

The rhyme in my head makes me smile, and I take a swig of my beer.

In another life, a long time ago when I was younger, I thought I could spit bars. But my footballing skills were a lot better than my rap lyrics.

Perhaps she didn't recognise me, after all. Maybe she only watches Premier League games which are broadcast more widely than other EFL leagues. The only people who usually recognise me are other footballers, journalists, or Viva City Panthers' fans.

I can't fault her. It's a free world. She's entitled to ignore me if she wishes. I'm not going to force myself on her.

The second half of the game restarts on the TV, and I focus on it. I chat occasionally with Faraji. He's a soccer fan who works in a sports bar. We have many things in common. He's in his thirties and has a wife and a young family. He asks me when I'll get married. It's a question I get a lot from my family. It seems a very popular question with Africans. I answer with the same flippancy I always use: "When I find the right person."

He tells me I shouldn't leave it too long because it is best to grow old with your family. I laugh it off because I'm only twenty-nine this year. I'm more interested in getting my soccer career back than finding a life partner.

My nape prickles occasionally, and when I glance at Ms Fuchsia, I catch her avoiding my gaze. She's been snooping at me. I hide my smile because it seems I'm now a distraction to her, as she was to me earlier.

But I don't approach her again. I respect her boundaries. The ball is in her court. If she wants me, she'll have to step out of the invisible wall she's built around herself and show it. Or at least wave a white flag.

My phone buzzes, and I check it. There are messages from Mak and Zafe. They are getting ready for the dinner party and are worried I wandered off.

I let out a sigh. There's no hiding from my obligations. I send quick replies and settle my bill.

Then I ask Faraji for a pen and paper. He slides them across the counter to me, and I scribble on the paper before passing it to him. "If the lady asks about me, give this to her. If she doesn't, put it in the bin."

"Okay. Take care, my friend," he says.

"And you, too, Faraji. Thank you for your help." I tip him generously and dismiss his effusive gratitude. He's been a lifesaver, and he doesn't realise it.

I walk into the warm evening, feeling light and bouncy. The golden sun disappears into the horizon, leaving streaks of orange and violet across the sky and ocean.

For the first time in days, perhaps weeks, I have a smile on my face as I go to meet my family and friends. I'm not afraid to face their questions about my wellbeing or football career. I don't know what the future holds, but I'm not ready to give up the fight just yet.

# 3

## Vivi

*Hi Tems, hope you're okay. I'm doing well. Zanzibar is beautiful. I can't lie. Wish you were here. I'm relaxing and staying off social media, as promised. The writing isn't going all that great, but I'm praying the inspiration comes. On the plus side, I'm reading a lot. Finished two books already. Sorry, got to go. The football match is about to start on the TV.*

*Message me back when you get a moment. Love, Vi* 🐸

A quick glance through the message, and I press send on my messaging app. Then I relax into my chair and glance up at the big screen on the far wall of the sports bar. I've been coming here daily since I arrived on the island three days ago.

My life spiralled after my attempt at proposing to Owen last Valentine's Day. He stormed out of his flat, leaving me on my knees in front of our friends and a livestream audience.

It felt like time stopped, and I froze in disbelief. Then the magnitude dawned, followed by a painful tightness in my throat. First, I cried, then I got angry. Sure, the whole thing was a surprise to him. But did he have to react so aggressively? Did he have to humiliate me like he did? This was a man I'd been in a relationship with for eighteen months prior. How did I miss the signs he wasn't into me for the long term?

Granted, he was my first serious relationship after university. My first...

Not my first kiss. I dated previously and shared kisses, but nothing more. Then I met Owen. I was just a girl from the 'Ends. And he was a football star from the EFL Championship. I fell for his charm hook, line, and sinker.

Kiru Taye

Was I naïve to think he cared about me?

That night, I left his house and took all my things. I didn't have too much stuff, just personal effects for when I stay overnight like a change of clothes and toiletries.

For a week, we didn't talk to each other. I was heartbroken and expected him to call and apologise for his behaviour. He didn't, and I was getting stressed out.

As a sportswriter, I usually write about other people's lives. Yet, now, I'm the one making headlines for the wrong reasons. A lot of the gossip rags have been running with the story. People calling me and asking if we're still dating, and I didn't even know the answer.

Then, about two weeks later, my phone rang. It was Owen. Angry, I ignored the call. Then he sent me a message:

**Why are you ignoring my calls?**

*Because I don't want to talk to you. You hurt my feelings and you still haven't apologised. You ignored me for 2 weeks.*

**I was upset. I needed a break.**

*You needed a break! Because I PROPOSED? You know what? Take an even longer BREAK.*

Enraged, I sent the message and blocked his number.

Temi suggested I take some time away as I had nothing major happening. Most of my work is freelance, anyway, although I have the *Loud and Proud* podcast. But we've recorded all the content for the upcoming episodes.

An editor I work regularly with asked me for the synopsis of my next article. However, this thing with Owen was screwing with my head, and I haven't been able to write anything since. I convinced him I would have something ready in two weeks. And I was hoping a break would provide inspiration.

Looking for an escape from the UK and my imploding life, I wanted somewhere far away without going to Australia. Zanzibar came up in the searches, and here I am. I wish my bestie was here with me, but she started a new job less than three months ago and can't take time off without notice.

The barman approaches and places the bottle of Smirnoff I ordered earlier and a glass on the table. "Here you go. Do you want any food tonight?"

"Thanks, Faraji. But not yet. I'll see how I feel when the game finishes." There's a food menu on the table, but I never eat food or snacks while watching a football match.

As a kid, I once saw a man choking on his pie while watching a game in the stadium. I think I was traumatised. A drink is the most I will consume during the match. In any case, all that munching is too much of a distraction when I want to concentrate.

"Okay. Let me know if you need anything else during halftime."

"I will. Thank you."

He returns to his perch behind the counter while I settle in for the game. He's been very kind to me since I started coming here three days ago. It's almost like he's adopted me and plays a big brother role.

The first night I was here, men were approaching me regularly, and I had to keep batting them away. It's as if a lone woman traveller has a target on her back and is easy pickings for them, made worse because I was the only woman in a sports bar, and a Black woman, too.

Faraji must have seen my discomfort at all the attention. When I arrived to watch the match yesterday, he'd set up this armchair in this corner by itself with just the table. It was so far away from the other seats that I might as well have a sign above me saying 'Leave her alone.'

When one man attempted to come over, Faraji called out and told him to stay away, that I was his cousin. I thanked him so much last night because I watched the full game with no hassles.

I'm hoping for the same luck today.

The match starts, and I get lost in the action. It's a Premier League game, and the two sides are evenly matched. I watch a lot of games for a living. As a sportswriter, I have to dig deep, give the scoop, and share stories that make fans feel connected to their favourite athletes and teams. I have to research athletes, teams, and their stories. My area of focus is soccer.

At half-time, I pop into the ladies quickly, then I return to my seat to check for messages on my phone as I don't check them during games either.

Faraji brings me another bottle of Smirnoff Ice. He already cleared the previous one when I emptied it into my glass. "The man at the counter paid for it already."

This surprises me, and I push the bottle back towards him. He knows I don't accept drinks from the men in this bar. "Take it back to whoever sent it."

I keep my gaze fixated on the large TV attached to a pillar at the end of the bar. The pundits are talking about what they expect from both teams in the second half.

Instead of taking the drink away like he's done before, Faraji leans down and speaks in the low tone. "He's not one of the others."

Curiosity sends tingles to the base of my neck. It seems the bartender approves of this person, considering he's been acting as my chaperone for three nights.

I tilt my head in the direction he indicates. My breath hitches. The face is instantly recognisable. But I squint because my eyes must be deceiving me.

Asher Uzodimma, the most capped player for Viva City Panthers FC, can't be in the same bar as me halfway across the world from the UK.

"Did he say his name?" I ask the barman in a rush of words.

"Asher Yuzodeema."

"Uzodimma," I correct him without thinking. My pulse accelerates.

"So, you know him," Faraji says excitedly.

"Tell him I said thank you." I don't want to discuss it. Nor do I want to be rude to the only

Black person at the bar, aside from the service staff.

The bartender nods and walks away.

I sneak another peek at the man who bought me a drink. His dark skin, his posture, his face. No doubt about it. I've seen him play too many times not to recognise him on sight.

I want to scream with excitement.

OMG! I'm in a bar with Asher Uzodimma, and he bought me a drink.

My hands are shaking, and I lower them onto my lap to hide them. Keeping my gaze on the screen, I shift in the seat, suddenly conscious of my clothing. My white shorts are tight and stop mid-thighs, and my tank-top clings to my breasts, making them appear bigger. My oversized shirt drapes over it all, keeping me modest. Does he find me attractive?

How did the two of us end up in the one location I chose to escape my life? Was he also trying to evade his life by coming here?

He hasn't played a match since the disastrous derby between DPR and VCP back in February when he sustained an injury. News reports said he would be out for at least eight weeks.

I replay the incident in my mind. Asher rolling on the ground, holding his leg, medics attending to him. DPR supporters booing him. At the time, I was one of those reprimanding him from the terraces because I thought his actions were malicious and designed to get Owen booked.

Now, regret scorches my cheeks because Owen was guilty of an atrocious tackle. Asher is still undergoing the impact of my ex's unsportsmanlike action. I can only hope it doesn't end the VCP player's career permanently. He is an outstanding athlete, and the league would miss his talent.

I didn't want any player injured. Not Asher, not anyone else. I simply wanted DPR to win the match against VCP. In the end, we drew two-all, and we haven't recovered in the league table since that day.

Now, Asher is sitting on a stool at the bar, barely eight metres from me. He bought me a drink and seems like a genuinely nice person since he hasn't attempted to approach me directly. I want to hide away because the last thing I want to reveal is that I dated the man who caused his injury.

Once the second half of the game starts, I fix my gaze on the large screen. Sneaking peeks at him at intervals, I turn away whenever he glances in my direction. My heart rate picks up slightly, my body temperature rising when he stares at me. Why do I feel like a teenager with a crush?

Nah. I shake out my shoulders. I can't have a crush on Asher Uzodimma.

First, there's the thing with Owen. Yes, we're on a break, which means we can both play away. A holiday fling would be acceptable.

But would Asher be a holiday fling? We live and work in the same city. What happens when he bumps into me at a sports event in London?

Second, he plays for Viva City Panthers, which is a rival to Duke's Park Rangers, and I'm a die-hard DPR fan. It will never work between us.

Third, Owen's tackle is the reason Asher isn't playing, and my regrets won't let me entertain anything friendly between us.

A flurry of second-half goals means I'm glued to the screen until the match ends. When I look at where Asher Uzodimma is sitting, he's no longer there.

I sit up and glance around.

Where did he go? Perhaps he went to the gents'.

Staying in the chair, I watch the door to the toilets. Several people go in and out. None of them are Asher.

My heart drops. Did he leave?

He bought me a drink and left? Wasn't he interested in me?

Okay. I didn't exactly invite him to talk to me. I was too busy analysing the pros and cons of having an affair with him in my head that I ignored him.

Shit.

I had the chance to talk to Asher Uzodimma, and I let him walk away?

Personal stuff aside, I'm still a professional, and I had the opportunity of a lifetime presented to me. What kind of sportswriter am I? I didn't even get to take a photo of him or even a selfie.

*Vivi, you messed up!*

I rub my hands over my face. How do I fix this? I don't even know which part of the resort he's staying in. What if he's leaving tomorrow?

Nausea rolls through me. This is not good.

I glance at Faraji, who is busy with customers. Perhaps he knows how to reach Asher. They were chatting for a while during the game.

I wait until he's served all the customers and it's quiet again. Then I walk over to the bar.

"Are you ready to order your food now?" he asks with a smile.

"Not yet," I reply. I lost my appetite, anyway. "I was wondering. You know the man that bought me a drink tonight. Asher Uzodimma. Do you know where he's staying? Or how to reach him?"

He frowns. "Why do you want to know? I thought you didn't like him."

"Oh, no. I like him," I rush to say and then realise what I've said as Faraji's face broadens in a smile. So, I add. "I mean, I know him as a talented footballer, and I wanted to speak to him after the game ended. You know I don't talk during a match. But when I wanted to talk to him, he was gone."

"I see." He's still smiling as if he knows something I don't. "He left something for you."

He pulls a folded lined paper out of his pocket and hands it to me.

"For me?" My heart races as I take it. Did Asher leave his phone number?

"Yes. He said I should give it to you only if you ask about him."

"Really?" My pulse skyrockets as I unfold the paper, my body trembling.

His handwriting is bold and printed. I scan through it and gasp. He's written a note and a poem.

Asher Uzodimma wrote me a poem. This is certainly a first for me. No one ever wrote me anything this creative. Or beautiful.

> **To my lady in fuchsia,**
>
> **I penned this note, for you're peng and dope.**
>
> **Meet me tomorrow and we'll make it a date.**
>
> **But if you're not here, I'll take it as fate.**
>
> **Yours, if you will, Asher.**

Warm spreads through me, and my smile blossoms. I could float as butterflies flutter in my belly.

"What does it say?" Faraji asks as he watches me.

"He asked me to meet him here for a date."

I can't believe I'm saying those words. Adrenaline spikes through me, making my skin warm and tingly. The note invokes a sense of being special, of being appreciated. It's a new sensation and a little scary.

"That's great. I think he's a good man. He needs a good woman like you."

I burst out with laughter, shaking my head. "How do you know he's a good man or that I'm a good woman?"

"Oh. I've seen you here for three days. I know you're a good woman. You're like my sister already, a member of my family. I want a good man for you. And Asher is a good man. I spoke to him."

"But how do you know he's a good man?" I persist, curious about how he came to that conclusion in the little time he spent with the man. I'm buzzing from seeing Asher, but it could be just hormones and attraction. Those are not a good indication of a decent person. Look at what happened with Owen.

"I know because—" he counts off his fingers "—he loves his family. He talked about them with such adoration. He flew all the way out here for a family event when he could have made an excuse about being injured."

"Okay," I acknowledge and wonder what family event it could be. Probably a wedding.

"He respects women," he continues. "You know he was not pushy like the other men, and he wasn't insulted because you didn't give him attention."

"That's true," I say. Asher could have taken my acceptance of his drink as an invitation to hassle me. But he didn't. "He was very respectful."

"And finally." He grins. "He is an amazing footballer. Case closed."

I chuckle. "Alright. Alright. I respect that."

"So, are you going to meet him tomorrow?"

"I'll think about it." I feign nonchalance. "So, what family event did Asher come here for?"

"It's his uncle's birthday, and there is a dinner party tonight. It's the reason he had to leave. They have a section of the resort reserved only for them. For about seventy-five people."

"All Nigerians?"

"Yes, I think so."

"Wow."

A customer orders a drink, and Faraji goes to serve him.

I stare at the note as a thought occurs to me. If Asher is here for a family event, it's possible he brought his friends, other sports stars. I don't have to wait until tomorrow when the real scoop could be happening tonight.

I want to see Asher again, but I also have the opportunity to put a hole in my writer's block. Hanging out with athletes for an evening could be the inspiration I need.

And if this is an event with Nigerian guests, then I'll blend in. These are my people. Worst-case scenario, I'll mention Asher's name to get in.

I bid Faraji goodnight and head back into the lobby where I board the lift going up to my room. In there, I shower, shave my legs, moisturise, apply make-up, style my hair. I don't know what the dress code is for the event, but I have a stylish white and pink maxi dress I bought for a special occasion. I wear it and match it with flat diamante sandals. My phone and hotel card are in my matching diamante purse with a long chain strap that goes across my shoulder.

Happy with my appearance in the full-length mirror, I head out and leave the hotel building. It's dark, and the promenade is lit by streetlamps and spotlights along the hedges. I walk along the beach, and the sea breeze is warm against my skin.

It isn't long before I hear the merrymaking, music, and conversations coming from the bar restaurant at the end of the pier. I walk towards

Kiru Taye

it. Before I can reach the entrance, two hefty men block my path.

"Are you here for the party?" one of them asks.

"Yes," I reply as my heart races. I wasn't expecting bouncers. But they look like serious security rather than casual workers. Interesting. These are heavy hitters. Who are they protecting? My pulse increases with the need to know, my inquisitive nature kicking in.

"What's your name?" The other one pulls out a tablet.

Oh, shit. They have a guest list. My name won't be on it.

"I'm with Asher Uzodimma," I blurt out before I can think better of it.

Shit, what if Asher already invited another guest to the party? I try not to fidget as excessive saliva fills my mouth with my agitation.

Please, I don't want to be kicked out before I get into the venue.

The man with the tablet looks through it and then at me. "I don't have a plus one for Asher Uzodimma."

Tension releases from my body unexpectedly. I do a mental fist pump that Asher didn't invite anyone else and roll with it. "It was a last-minute invitation. Maybe he forgot to mention it to you guys."

"Wait here," the first one says and walks away.

My heart races, and my skin flushes hot and cold as I stand there under the scrutiny of the security guard. Let's hope Asher doesn't get me booted out.

# 4

## Asher

It turns out my fears are unfounded after I shower, change, and turn up for the dinner party later than everyone else. The restaurant is at the end of a long pier floating over the ocean. The place sits at least a hundred people, and it's practically full, the party swinging.

We are Nigerians. When we show up, the world must notice.

The second I walk in, I am embraced and showered with greetings and well wishes from every relative I encounter as I walk deeper into the venue. I have to go around the tables and greet everyone I know, and they, in turn, introduce me to any guests they invited.

One of my aunts, who is a pastor, interrupts the party and makes me kneel on the floor. She proceeds to say a prayer over my bowed head, casting and binding every evil intent and returning it to the sender. She prays for me to endure this trial with fortitude, for the injury to heal quickly, and for me to be renewed with vigour. Predicting my future, she even prophesies that I'll be playing in the Premier League next season. Everybody present choruses in a very loud, "Amen!"

"It is well with you," she says and releases her hand from my head.

"Thank you, Aunty," I say, rising to my feet and smiling like a loon. The darkness lifts from me, and I am reminded of the things I enjoy. There is nothing quite like the pleasure of being with family and friends. The fun of parties.

The stage is reserved for the live band rather than the guest of honour, as in other Nigerian functions.

There are no special mentions or chairperson. There is no need. Everyone here is special because they are family and close friends. Everybody is blinging.

The decorations, white brocade linen and flowers, are amazing. The party planners have done very well.

In the middle of the restaurant, the celebrant is with his wife, brother, and sister-in-law, also known as Sister Tari's parents, and they sit together at a round table. My big aunt, Mrs Duru, is also there, along with an older gentleman and a couple I don't recognise.

I go over and greet everyone at the table, starting with Chief Essien. Although he's an uncle-in-law, I call him Daddy because Zafe calls him Daddy. In truth, he's like a godfather to many of us here who are not his direct blood.

My mother has told me stories about how he stepped up and ensured Sis Ebony and her mother were protected after her husband and only son died in a car crash. In those days, some members of the Duru family were trying to take away their Lagos properties because 'women don't inherit properties' according to them. Although Mrs Duru had been disabled because of the same accident that cost her husband's and son's lives, she wasn't a pushover, and she fought them in the courts and won. According to my mum, Chief Essien threatened to lock up anyone who harassed Mrs Duru.

That was over thirty years ago.

The setup positions the middle table as the focal point, with the other round tables surrounding it in a circle.

I turn towards the occupants of the next table.

"Sister Ebony, Bro Felix, good evening." I bow in greeting.

"Asher, good evening. It's been a while." She rises and hugs me as her husband stands, too.

"How are you?" he asks as he gives me a side hug.

"I'm well, thank you. You guys look amazing."

They wear matching white linen with gold embroidery at the hems and collars. Looking fresh for a couple in their mid-forties, even if there are speckles of salt with the pepper of their hair.

In fact, everyone here looks amazing.

"Thank you, Asher. You remember Alex." She points at the fourteen-year-old boy who has a gaming console in his hand.

"Hello, Alex," I say when he comes over, giving him a hug, too. "Where are your sisters?" He has younger twin sisters aged ten.

"Hello, Uncle Asher," he replies. "They are playing. I'll find them."

I pull out a chair and sit with Bro Felix and Sis Ebony while they ask about my parents and siblings. They enquire about my health and express wishes of speedy recovery. Bro Felix even suggests introducing me to another sports medic if I need a different opinion about my prognosis. Once the energetic twins Pearl and Megan arrive, they practically follow me around as I finish the round of greetings.

I make it to the bar and order a drink. Mak is propping up the bar and moping like a boy who lost his favourite toy. The thing with Ranti is not going well because he keeps staring at her, and she keeps ignoring him.

It reminds me of my encounter with Lady in Fuchsia at the sports bar. Will I see her again? Will she accept the invitation to meet tomorrow? My pulse accelerates at the thought of seeing her again.

But did she even read the note?

I shake my head and pat Mak's shoulder in sympathy before heading over to Uncle Freddie's and Aunt Kike's table.

Confused about the naming conventions? Let me back up and explain. In our extended family, there is no hard and fast rule about the way we address the elders. The only rule applies to the way we relate to them rather than how old they are.

It's just a Nigerian thing or an African thing, perhaps.

So, for example, Chief Essien is Daddy because I've always called him Daddy and his son is my friend.

Sis Ebony is Sis, because she's like a big sister to me. She is my blood cousin and older than me by fifteen years. So, I can't call her by her first name only.

In the same vein, Bro Felix is Bro because he is married to Sis Ebony, get it?

Uncle Freddie is different because although he is technically Bro Freddie to me, we've always called him Uncle Freddie. He is Ranti's father, and Ranti is in our—me, Zafe, Inna and Mak's—age group, and we all used to hang out when we were younger. Therefore, he is a father figure to us rather than an older sibling. Hence Uncle Freddie. Makes sense, right?

Anyway, Ranti and Inna are also at the table, and we get into a gist about everything and anything as I eat the meal.

"I hear you guys helped to decorate this place. It's wonderful," I say after I finish eating.

"Yes, we have skills," Ranti jokes and stands. "I'm going to get some more drinks for the table."

When she leaves, Inna and I catch up on life. She is a junior doctor, living in the US. She talks about her stressful life with all the studying and exams she must take to practise over there, although she has already qualified in Nigeria.

"Uh-oh," she says, interrupting the conversation. "This is not good."

"What is it?"

She points towards the bar, and I look up.

Ranti is walking back to the table with the tray of drinks while Uncle Freddie is having what looks like a stern word with Mak. No, it's not good.

When Uncle Freddie heads back to the table, I excuse myself and go to Mak. He looks dejected, and I feel for him. I try to find out what really went on between him and Ranti, but he clams up.

"Asher, can I talk to you?"

Bro Kola steps up to me. He is ex-military and has this authoritative expression that can put the fear of God into anyone.

"Sure, what is it?" I ask, wondering what I've done wrong.

"Come with me."

I follow him outside into the warm night. The sound of the ocean mixes with the music from inside. One of the bodyguards is waiting there.

"Did you invite anyone to the party?" Bro Kola asks.

I frown and glance from one to the other. "No. What is this about?"

"There is a woman at the bottom of the pier who says you invited her to the party."

"Oh." The only woman I've met on the island is Ms Fuchsia. "Can I go down there and see her?"

"I've got her photo here." The security man pulls out his phone and swipes the screen before passing it to me.

I glance at the screen, and my heart jolts. Although the photo is dark, I recognise the woman from the sports bar at once. "Yes, I know her. Can you let her in, please?"

Bro Kola stares at me for a moment, and I think he is going to decline my request. Then he turns to the guard. "Chibby, please go down and escort the lady up here."

The guard nods and walks away.

Bro Kola's gaze stays on me, and I shift, staring into the inky depths of the ocean. I lied to him, so of course I'm uncomfortable. I'm not used to telling lies to people I care about. People who care about me.

"How do you know the woman?" he asks eventually.

My cheeks heat.

"That's a little too personal." I fidget with my collar.

He steps closer and gets in my face, but keeps his voice low. "There is a reason we have a guest list. I don't joke about the wellbeing of these family members. Security has vetted and cleared everybody here. If you're going to pick up street girls, then you shouldn't bring them to a family function. I thought you'd outgrown your teenage recklessness. Asher, you should know better than this."

His voice rises toward the end.

I want to tell him I *have* outgrown my teenage wildness, but a gasping noise behind me makes me swivel.

Ms Fuchsia is standing there, her mouth agape. She must have overhead part of Bro Kola's rant.

My ears and face burn hot. I wish the ground would swallow me whole because he revealed my wild past to the woman I am trying to win over. I've done some stupid things, things I'm ashamed to admit.

Meeting Lady in Fuchsia is different. For reasons I can't explain fully. It's just a gut feeling, an instinct.

However, the grimace on her face and her throat rippling as she swallows repeatedly telegraphs her discomfort. It propels me into action, my embarrassment shoved aside. I won't have anyone talk down to her. I have to do something to save her face, before my family and friends mark her as a street girl.

She started this by showing up here without an invitation, and now, I have to salvage the situation. Even if it means putting myself in the firing line.

"It's not like that. I know different." I walk over to her and extend my hand towards her, hoping she'll take it. "She is my girlfriend. I forgot to let security know she was on the island and would attend tonight. I'm sorry about that."

# 5

*Vivi*

The security men make me wait at least ten minutes. The one who went away earlier returns and tells me to stay. Someone will be with me shortly.

I pace back and forth along the beach. Anyone would think they were guarding royalty. Is Asher's uncle a king or something? They booked out half a resort, so it's more than possible.

Huffing, I keep pacing. I'm more curious to find out who these people are. Imagine the potential content I can spin out of this when I get into the venue. There will be material for a newspaper story, visuals for social media, and gossip for my podcast audience.

A man jogs down the promenade to me. A third security man in a suit and tie.

"Ms, come with me," he says and doesn't wait for my response before walking back briskly.

I follow at a fast pace to keep up with him. The crashing waves mask our footsteps. There is a slight incline, and you don't see the entrance to the restaurant until you turn the corner.

Asher is standing outside talking with another man in low voices. It's obvious they don't hear us approach because of the music and waves.

Asher wears a cream linen tunic and trouser set with intricate embroidery around the collar and hems. On his feet are gold-trimmed monogrammed loafers. The gold watch on his wrist catches the light.

The tunic showcases his broad back and shoulders. As he's standing, it's obvious how tall he is, how magnificent and royal. He is hot, and that's just his back.

I move closer but halt when I hear what the man is saying to him.

"…If you're going to pick up street girls, then you shouldn't bring them to a family function. I thought you'd outgrown your teenage recklessness. Asher, you should know better than this."

A loud gasp escapes me. Are they talking about me?

Asher swivels and faces me. The guilt-ridden expression on his face confirms my suspicions.

WTH! This bald-headed uncle didn't just call me a street girl.

Just because I showed up at their party uninvited. Who the hell do they think they are? I've never been so embarrassed in my life.

A tingle sweeps from the back of my neck across my face. I swallow repeatedly to clear my throat and cough. I want to disappear and hide in shame. Yet, I also want to get into the uncle's face and tell him to go to Hell.

But I'm a tourist, far away from home. They have an entire family. A whole fucking army.

Best to tuck my tail in and crawl back into the hole I came from because I know when I'm outgunned and out-manned. I have no one to protect me here.

But Asher speaks up as he walks towards me. "It's not like that. I know different."

He holds out his hand and stares into my eyes as he speaks. "She is my girlfriend. I forgot to let security know she was on the island and would attend tonight. I'm sorry about that."

What? For a few seconds, I'm too dazed to speak, to respond.

While staring into my eyes, his expression imploring and apologetic, he talks to the older man. He is trying to communicate with me, coming to my rescue and standing up for me.

Why? He doesn't have to. He doesn't know me. We haven't even spoken directly to each other before. Our communication was through Faraji. Then he wrote me a poem, and I showed up here.

He owes me nothing. Yet, he is helping me. Trying to save my face in front of these men.

He breaks eye contact and looks down at his hand hanging in the air between us while I analyse his actions. Just like earlier this evening, when I ignored him after he bought me a drink.

He is giving me a lifeline. A second chance. Just like he did with his note.

Throwing caution to the wind, I put my hand in his, and tingles shoot down my arm.

"I thought you weren't going to make it," he says and closes his warm palm around mine.

He's still looking at me like there's no one else around. It's a little intense, but I like it.

"I'm sorry I'm late," I say aloud, playing the part of a tardy girlfriend.

He leans in and kisses my cheek. Then he whispers into my ear, "What's your name?"

Oh, shit. He doesn't know my name. Good thing no one asked him because this wouldn't have worked.

"Vivi," I reply in a whisper into his ear as I lean up and hug him to make it look like we're embracing.

He places his hand around my back, turning me to face the other man. "Bro Kola, this is Vivi. Vivi … Bro Kola. He is one of my uncle's sons."

"It's nice to meet you, sir. I'm sorry for the hassle I caused." In my attempt to be civil, I understand the man's approval is necessary for me to enter the venue. I must go in there and see the rest of this *royal* family for myself.

After I suffered all the insults, I must have evidence for prime gist. Otherwise, no one will believe I gate-crashed one Chief Daddy's birthday party in Zanzibar.

The Bro Kola scrutinises me for a second before responding. "You're welcome. Chibby is going to scan you and check your purse before you can go inside."

"Oh." I glance at Asher with a frown.

"It's okay." He squeezes my hand and steps away, but he doesn't release my hand as the security man waves his scanning wand around me. He only lets go briefly so the guard can wave it down my sides.

Then I open my purse, and the man flashes a torch into it and checks the contents before saying, "All clear."

"You can go in now," Bro Kola says.

"Thank you." Asher holds my hand as we walk inside.

The place is bright and packed full of partygoers, young and old and middle-aged. On the stage is a man giving tribute to the celebrant, Chief Essien. I recognise him. That is Mak Phillips, another footballer who plays in the Italian Serie A league. My gaze bounces around the place until I find Zafe Essien, who is also a soccer player in Italy.

Then it clicks. Zafe must be Chief Essien's son. And Asher must be related to the old man, too. I need to determine how Mak is connected to them, as well.

I just hit the jackpot. This could be the biggest scoop of my life.

"What do you want to drink?"

I blink as I realise Asher is talking to me. We're standing next to the bar.

"I probably shouldn't drink more alcohol without eating," I say.

"You haven't eaten?" He looks surprised.

"No. I don't eat when I'm watching football, and afterwards, I went to my room to get ready to come here."

He leans his side against the counter, facing me. "Which reminds me. Why are you here?"

This catches me off-guard. Doesn't he want me here? I tug my hand free from his. "Don't you want me here?"

"That's not what I said."

He reaches for my hand again, and I pull it back.

"You invited me on a date."

"Tomorrow evening. Not tonight. Tonight is for family."

"And I'm not."

It's like a sucker punch in the gut with the realisation. Although it's not supposed to hurt so much, it does. It's an echo of the pain from Owen's rejection.

"I don't mean it that way. Look, let me get you something to eat. Nike," he calls a young woman who must be in her late teens. "Can you check with the caterers and see if there's food left for my guest?"

"Okay, Brother. I'll check." She walks away.

I glance around the venue, and everyone is so relaxed, so familiar with each other. They look like nice people.

I'm the outsider. The one chasing a scoop for my career. For clicks and bants.

The nonsense with Owen has made me erect walls around myself. Made me less willing to get involved with another man. Made me more hard-nosed?

But Asher Uzodimma doesn't deserve to be used as fodder to feed my online followers. To grow my career. He's been nothing but a gentleman, protective, respectful, even romantic.

Faraji wasn't a good judge of character. Because I'm not worthy of Asher.

If sex is all he wants, then good. But he behaves like a man who wants more from me than I can give him. More than I'm willing to give him. I shouldn't be here.

I straighten. "I should go."

"Go? Why?" He frowns as he stares into my eyes.

"I'm sorry for gatecrashing the party and making you lie to your family about me."

I try to look away, but he cups my cheek gently, holding my gaze.

"I don't care about that—"

"Bro Asher, here's the food." The young lady returns with a platter of food, interrupting us.

"That's a lot," I comment.

"I didn't know what you wanted, so I brought a bit of everything," she replies.

"See, we're bribing you with food. Please stay," Asher teases.

I giggle as my stomach rumbles. I'm hungry. "Okay, I'll stay."

"Yes!" he cheers and directs me to a table with other people close to our age and introduces them. The group includes Zafe Essien soccer trophy winner, Tony Essien award-winning movie producer, Rita Essien, award-winning actress, Joel Ali, award-winning director, and others. Mak Phillips is no longer here.

Still, I'm among superstars. These are the elites in their fields. And as they talk, they all seem down to earth, like normal humans. The only difference between us is the number of zeros in their bank accounts and the number of trophies in their cabinets.

Nike leaves the food on the table, and I thank her. A server brings a bottle of wine and pours a glass for me.

"I can't finish this, so you're going to have to join me," I say to Asher.

Smiling, he picks up the cutlery and joins in. The platter contains almost everything: grilled fish and prawns, fried plantain, Asaro, Nkwobi, Jollof rice, Abacha salad. This is the taste of home away from home.

The party winds down, and the elders and those with little children leave. The group at our table stay and chat football. I listen to them while I eat.

"Do you watch football?" Joel asks me when I finish eating.

Asher bursts into laughter. "This one. You want to ask her if she watches football? This one loves football die."

The men around the table grin. "Really?"

"Yes," I reply. "I do more than watch. I actually play, too. When I was a teenager, I tried out for one of the major teams, but I didn't get scouted."

"Oh." Asher looks at me as if seeing me for the first time.

"That's a shame," Tony comments.

"Yeah. But I still play for my local five-a-side team."

"Okay. So, which team do you support?"

This is a trap. There's no way I can mention Duke's Park Rangers without causing wahala with Asher. So, I chose a different club.

"Manchester City." It's not a lie. I do support Man City. The only time I don't support them is when they play against DPR during the FA Cup tournament. When DPR gets promoted into the Premier League, I will have to make Man City my backup team.

The men at the table groan and poke fun at Asher.

"You could have said Viva City Panthers, you know, and spared my ego." Asher shakes his head as he smiles.

"Yeah, well. I only support winning teams," I tease back.

"Shots fired!" Zafe hollers and drums on the table.

"Ouch!" Asher clutches his chest as if I've mortally wounded him. But his eyes sparkle with humour. "You're brutal."

"And yet you like me," I say, tilting my head to stare into his eyes.

Although I'm teasing him, I'm serious. I want him to like me. I've only been with him for a few hours, yet I feel a release, a freedom I never experience with Owen. Some of Owen's friends are downright condescending, which is why I don't enjoy hanging with them, anyway.

Yet, amongst these strangers, these acquaintances, I feel like I've made lifelong friends. They laugh and joke with me rather than at me. I'm not the butt of their jokes. I'm not the outsider.

Asher is doing this thing again when he looks at me and the world disappears. It's just me and him.

"Yes, I do," he says, all serious.

Suddenly, I want to cry. I want to tell him he shouldn't like me. I'm so wrong for him for so many reasons. For one, I came here to get a scoop. He'll hate me when he sees his name splashed across the sports pages.

Which is as well because I'm not ready to date anyone else.

So why am I sitting here, hanging onto his every word? Why does his gaze heat my skin?

Why does his touch set my pulse racing and his smile fill me with warmth?

I'm so enamoured with him, I haven't bothered to take photos with him or the other celebrities. What is going on with me?

As if sensing my turmoil, he stands and holds out his hand. "Come on. Let's go for a walk."

"It's midnight," I protest, feeling warm and cosy in here. Also, I shouldn't leave without the photos for the article.

"It's tomorrow, and we have a date," he counters, his voice deep and seductive.

"Of course, we do." I smile and take his outstretched hand. "Good night, everyone. It was nice to meet you."

"Good night, Vivi," they chorus, more or less, and I follow my date into the night.

## Asher

The night is still warm as I step outside the restaurant on the pier, Vivi a step behind me. The sound of the crashing waves against the shore provides a background cadence now the music has stopped.

On the wooden decking, I pause and breath in the briny breeze.

She stands beside me and fidgets with her purse, a frown creasing her face.

Her face is very expressive. I don't know if she realises it.

"What's the problem?" I turn to her, discovering that I don't like to see her in discomfort. It seems to be an automatic reaction with her. I want to demolish anything that bothers her.

"Do you mind if I take a selfie?" she asks, biting her bottom lip.

"Of course not." I want to oblige her requests and fulfil her wishes. I move closer to her. "Do you want it out here?"

"I mean inside. With your cousins. You know, the guys at our table."

I angle my body away as my stomach knots with suspicion. "Why?"

"Well, I met all these famous people, and I have no proof that I met them," she says in a blasé tone.

"But you don't know them that well, and this is not a public event," I say, testing her.

The Essien family has a history of people trying to take advantage of their generosity.

"Yeah. But I was here. I met all these celebrities. I need proof. Otherwise, my cousin Temi won't believe that I was actually here."

It sounds like she's saying I won't see her after tonight. Like taking the photo is goodbye. A chill passes over me.

"And what will you do with them? Will you post the photos on social media?"

She rolls her eyes. "Well, duh? That's the whole point."

My stomach clenches, and my ribs squeeze tight.

"So that's why you came here. It wasn't because of me. It was so you could find some gossip." I can't hide my disappointment. "Bro Kola was right. I was stupid to trust you. And there I was thinking you came here to see me."

I shake my head and storm off down the embarkment, my mind in turmoil. I can't believe I was such an idiot. To think I genuinely like her, and yet, her interest in me was for entertainment of her online followers. Maybe she will even sell the photos to a media house.

"No, Asher, wait!" she calls out, and I can hear her footsteps behind me.

I jerk to a halt and swivel. "You know what? You want a photograph? Let's go back so you can take the goddamn photo."

"No!" she shouts.

"Why not?" I counter.

"Not if it's going to make you this angry."

I turn again and resume stomping down the pier towards the shore.

"Asher, stop. Let me explain."

"What's there to explain?" I stop but don't turn. "Did you or did you not come here to gather information to publish online?"

She stops in front of me and says in a soft voice while reaching for my hand. "I did."

I pull back.

"Please listen to me. When I found out that you were attending a family event on the island, I was curious. About you and your family. So, I decided to come here. Initially, my interest was about a quick tabloid headline like: *Injured VCP winger spotted partying in Zanzibar while the team struggles with crucial matches*."

My breath hitches. This woman is mercenary, opportunistic, and mean.

"But then I arrived and saw how nice you were to me. You defended me when I was the one who messed up. Your family members were nice to me. Even Bro Kola was just being protective towards you and the rest of the family. Anyway, I had so much fun tonight. I didn't even remember to take any photos, which is unlike me.

"As we were leaving, it occurred to me I can change the focus of my story. I'm a sportswriter. Instead of the tabloid headline, I can write a human-interest story. You are a pivotal player in the EFL Championship, and Viva City Panthers are fighting for promotion to the Premier League. I was thinking of writing a story about you, your relationship with your family and the important role they played in motivating you through your recovery. That's when it occurred to me I still didn't have any photos of you or your family. The ones at our table are already famous people in the public eye. I didn't think there would be any problem taking a photo with them."

Her explanation makes sense and gives me pause.

"So, you don't want to sell the photos to a tabloid or gossip mag?"

"No. I won't do that to you. Not after how wonderfully you treated me tonight."

I puff out air and allow relief to wash over me. But my relief doesn't last long because the bodyguards walk towards us. We're standing near the entrance of the pier where they are stationed for the night.

"Asher, I have to detain your guest," one of them says. The other is talking into a mobile phone at his ear.

"Detain who?" I ask as I instinctively push Vivi behind me. I know what's coming, but I'm not about to let them touch her. They must have overhead our argument.

He points at Vivi.

"What?" she gasps, eyes widening.

"Are you mad? You are not detaining her. She is my girlfriend." I step back, keeping her behind me so they can't touch her.

"Boss wants us to make sure she hasn't recorded anything from the party," the one on the phone says.

Boss is Bro Kola. He owns the security firm, and these are his employees.

"I want to speak to him," I demand.

The bodyguard hands the phone over.

"Bro Kola, this is not fair," I say without preamble. "This is harassment. How many other people did they detain and search as they left the venue?"

"Your girlfriend—" he spits those words out with vehemence "—is a journalist who just confessed to coming to the venue to bag a story. The bodyguards have every right to ensure she doesn't violate the privacy of the people in attendance."

He's correct. Our family's privacy is important.

"But she said she didn't take any photos or videos."

"And you believe her?"

"Yes, I believe her!"

Silence hangs on the line for a few seconds before he speaks. "Let me make this very clear. Are you willing to risk the free pass you have to family events? Because if gossip or newspaper story is printed without permission, you will suffer the consequences."

I know what he is referring to.

When Sis Ebony was newly wed to Bro Felix, I went to stay with them for a few weeks, and Bro Kola found a girl I snuck into my bedroom. For punishment, he barred me from inviting friends to the house. Even my male friends couldn't visit. Can you imagine being a teenager and your friends can't visit you? That was hard.

From what he is saying now, he can bar me from inviting guests to future Essien family events.

All because of Vivi.

Can I really swear she will not go to the tabloids like she originally wanted?

I turn, scrutinising her tight expression. There's fear and anxiety and pleading there.

I hate that she's backed into a corner like this. Sure, she started out wanting to use me. But I believe she changed her mind. I believe she's sincere.

"I'm willing to risk the consequences. She will not publish anything without permission." As I speak, I hold her gaze so she understands the gravity of my words.

If she publishes anything that isn't authorised, I will get ostracised from the Essien family gatherings.

"Okay." Bro Kola heaves a heavy sigh on the phone. "Good night, Asher."

"Good night, Bro Kola." I hand the phone back to the bodyguard.

He listens to the boss's instructions and then says, "You can go."

I take Vivi's hand, and we hurry down the promenade and onto the beach. I don't feel much like the midnight stroll I originally planned on. The mood has been killed.

She doesn't say anything, and we walk silently for a while.

"Do you want to go back to your room?" I ask.

She glances at me tentatively, looking uncertain and vulnerable for the first time tonight. "Do you want me to go?"

I scrub a hand over my face. The last thirty minutes have been a roller coaster of emotions since leaving the restaurant and she confessed her intentions. I'm drained and tired.

"I'll go." She tries to tug her hand free, but I don't let go.

The thought of letting her go leaves my chest aching. "I don't want you to go."

She nods, and we start walking again. We go down the paved tree-lined street towards the thatched bungalow. The other villas are quiet, the occupants probably asleep.

When we reach the veranda, I take her to the hammock tied to four posts in the corner instead of indoors.

I'm sharing a room with Mak, so I can't take her in there, anyway.

Lifting her onto the hammock, I slide off her sandals.

"I'll be back in a minute," I say and walk to the front door. Opening it gently in case someone is asleep in the living room, I enter and grab the throw and a couple of cushions before returning to the veranda.

"Here." I give her the cushion, hop onto the hammock beside her and kick off my loafers.

"Are we going to sleep out here?" she asks.

"We can watch the stars out here," I reply. It was on the resort website.

"Very romantic," she says with a smile.

Without replying, I wrap an arm around her and tip our bodies, so we're lying with her tucked into me. I tug the throw over our clothed forms. I want to get naked with her so badly. But I'm being cautious. I have to be careful. Family aside, I still have a career to protect. There are too many sex tapes floating around the internet by people looking for their fifteen minutes of fame.

We stare at the starry night sky. It is beautiful and worth sleeping outside to experience.

"You're still angry with me," she says in a soft voice. She sounds uncertain, too.

A sigh escapes me. "I'm not angry. I'm … tired … conflicted. I staked a lot for you tonight. I could alienate my family and friends because of you."

She leans against my chest and lifts her head to look at my face in the dark. The movement sways the hammock. "Thank you for coming to my rescue tonight. Twice. You are an amazing man."

"Why do I feel as if me being amazing is not enough for you?"

It's her turn to sigh as she lies back against me. "My life is complicated right now."

She doesn't say more, and I don't push her. I guess a part of me is afraid of pushing and sending her away. But I feel the inexplicable connection between us. It's intoxicating.

"Promise me you won't publish anything about my uncle's birthday party," I say eventually.

"I promise," she whispers.

I turn and press my lips to her temple. "Thank you."

Soon afterwards, I hear the gentle sighs indicating she's asleep. I doze off and wake when she stirs, requesting to use the bathroom. I take her inside and show her. When she's done, I use it, too, before we return to the hammock.

When dawn finally arrives, Vivi is still tucked in by my side as the birds recite the morning song.

## 7

## Vivi

It takes a few seconds to get my bearing when I open my eyes the next morning. The sky has a tinge of grey, but it's not quite daylight yet. The sound of the sea waves gently rolling onto the beach reaches me from only metres away.

A cool breeze makes me snuggle deep into the warmth surrounding me. I'm cradled by solid muscles—Asher—his right arm around me, a soft grey blanket over us. We're lying on a hammock bed outside the holiday villa he's sharing with his footballing friends.

Well, I say a hammock and you probably imagine a net bed tied to two trees. However, this is a raised wooden frame lined with a soft mattress and cushions. Four ropes tie it to the canopy held up by four posts carved from thick tree trunks in each corner. The ceiling has a woven gauze-like appearance, which allows us to view the sky while providing shelter. The surrounding trees and shrubs provide shade and seclusion.

We slept out here last night and watched the covering of silver twinkling stars in the cobalt sky. It was beautiful, magical, romantic.

I've never done anything like it before.

Emotions suddenly choke my throat. I suck in a deep breath, taking in the faint scent of his cologne and musk. I remember yesterday. From the moment I met Asher at the sports bar, I've been riding a rollercoaster wave.

It's been amazing and scary because despite all the drama I caused. Yes, I caused them. I know myself and my life. But he has been so grounded, so calm, so graceful and forgiving.

I don't know this man. Not really. I haven't even spent twenty-four hours with him. Yet, I can feel the pull of attraction. Not just physically because damn he'd hot and hard, and snuggled up to him like this while he sleeps brings it into sharp focus.

The attraction, I can handle.

It's the rest that has me rattled. Has me fumbling and making rookie mistakes.

Because why in hell did I confess my intentions to him last night? If I hadn't mentioned the real reason I showed up to his family get-together, I'm sure he would have allowed me to take the photograph with his cousins and friends. He would not have known my intent until the article was published.

Now I have no photograph to show that I really was here with him.

But I have him. Isn't that enough?

I huff out a sigh.

After the shenanigans with Owen, I told myself I didn't want a man, didn't need a man. Because Owen Price hurt me in a way I've never experienced before.

And honestly, I don't want to care about another man. I have my blossoming career to focus on.

So, what is this thing with Asher?

Why am I curled up beside him on a hammock, listening to the sound of the waves only metres away? Why did I spend the night with him without having sex?

Lying here with him like this is more intimate than having sex.

I've hung around enough sports people to understand the ego and libido associated with them. So, to be with one who isn't trying to get into my knickers is surprising.

What does he want from me if not lust and pleasure?

He wrote me a poem the first time we met, so I can guess he's seeking something more substantial. Something out of my power to give.

I should end this now. Get out of his embrace and walk back to my hotel before everyone else wakes up and sees me do the walk of shame.

Last night when he asked if I wanted to return to my room, I should have said yes. But I experienced a constricting feeling in my chest in dismay that he didn't want me. I didn't want our parting to be on an unpleasant note after he convinced the security men to not search me.

I'm confused. I'm not sure I've ever been conflicted about a man, Owen notwithstanding.

Is the heart smart enough to choose who it cares about?

I don't know the answer.

I shift and try to roll to the edge of the hammock. But Asher's grip tightens on me, and I land back half on him and half off.

"Good morning." His voice is deep and husky from sleep.

I tilt my head to look up at his face, and my heart jolts because he has a dreamy smile. His dark eyes glimmer in the dawn light, mesmerising me, filling me with urges I can't explain.

"Morning," I croak and swallow hard.

He leans in, kisses my cheek and the corner of my mouth. Tingles shoot down my face to my nipples. The urge to rub against him grows. To feel his hands on my skin.

A squeaking sound makes me freeze. Someone is coming outside.

He sighs and lies back as the door opens and someone in shorts and a T-shirt steps out.

I recognise Mak Phillips. I hadn't seen him after he made a speech last night. I thought he would've been at the table with the other guys.

"Sorry, I didn't know you were out here," Mak says and turns to head back inside. "Oh, reminder, we're going on a tour after breakfast this morning."

"A tour?" Asher shifts to the edge of the hammock and sits up. The white vest stretches across his broad back, showing off his bare, tattooed arms. He removed the tunic he wore yesterday but is still wearing the trousers.

"Yes," Mak replies. "Ranti organised a visit around some of the tourist sites in Stone Town. We're all going."

"We?" Asher glances back and reaches for my hand. "Oh, I don't think you two have met. Mak, this is Vivi."

"Nice to meet you, Mak." I shuffle to the edge beside Asher.

"Same here. Vivi is welcome to join us. We're all meeting in the restaurant for breakfast. Then the tour starts afterwards."

"I don't know if I can make it," I say.

"I would love you to join us. Did you have something else planned?" Asher asks.

I frown. "No. But I've intruded enough on your family time."

"I don't think you're intruding. And Mak—" he waves at his friend, "—doesn't think you're intruding."

"No, I don't." Mak sounds amused. "As I said, you are welcome to join us, Vivi. In fact, I think it will be a great idea because if you don't join us, my friend Asher will be very miserable. So please, join us."

I can't help laughing.

How is it possible that these guys are so down to Earth. So genuine. These are soccer stars. The rockstars of African football. The ones who make women and men swoon on sight.

Yet, I spent the night with one and am now making jokes with another. And they are not misbehaving. This is heaven. A dream I didn't know I had coming to pass.

"Okay. I'll tag along. But I need to get back to my room first." I'm suddenly conscious of my appearance. My hair must be a basket mess since I didn't cover it with the net or wrap. My makeup will be smudged and all over the place. Never mind my rumpled dress.

"Yeah. I'll come with you," Asher says and hops off the hammock. "I'll pack the things to change into."

"It'll be quicker if you take the electric buggy." Mak points at the golf cart type vehicle parked at the edge of the bungalow. It's plugged into a charging point.

"Good idea." Asher places his hands around my waist and lifts me off the hammock.

We head into the house.

"Do you mind if I use the bathroom?" I ask.

"Sure." He waves at the door as he heads into his bedroom.

I use the bathroom quickly and tidy up my appearance as best I can.

When I come out, he's ready with a small gym bag. We head outside, and after a few seconds trying to figure out how the buggy works, we're on our way. Less than five minutes later, he parks it outside the hotel lobby with the valets. We go inside and into the lift.

In my room, he lets me go in the shower first which is only fair. I strip off, wrap my hair, and cover it with a shower cap before going under the spray. I scrub every part of my body as excitement rolls through me.

Asher Uzodimma is in my bedroom. Sure, we didn't get down and dirty last night. But nothing stops us from getting down and dirty this morning. I'm not about to let the opportunity go to waste.

This could be the last chance to be with him. I'm back in the UK soon, and I don't know when he's going back. Once we land in London, we can never be in contact except maybe in a professional setting.

After rinsing the suds off, I switch off the faucet and grab the white bathrobe which covers me from neck to ankles. I brush my teeth and then check myself in the mirror over the sink. Happy with the face staring back at me, I open the door and step out.

It occurs to me the door wasn't locked and he could have come inside the bathroom while I was in the shower. A seed of doubt is planted in my mind. What if he's not really attracted to me? What if...?

"Great," he says, looking up from his phone when he sees me.

He grabs his bag and walks around me. "I won't be long."

Then he enters the bathroom and shuts the door.

I stand there for a few seconds, doubt warring with desire. I could open the door and go in after him. There would be no mistaking what I want if I take off the robe and he sees me naked.

But I'm not about to put my emotional and psychological wellbeing to the test.

After Owen rejected my proposal so brutally, I can't trust myself to make the first move. I dated

Owen for almost two years and didn't see his rejection coming. I don't know Asher well enough to predict how he will behave.

And the insult of throwing myself at another man who doesn't want me will be too much to bear.

I go to the wardrobe and grab a pair of wide leg multi print trousers and match it with a ruffled matching fuchsia top with ruffled sleeves. I start on my makeup, keeping it minimal, then I stand in front of the full-length mirror, brushing my hair. Thankfully, it's not too tangled, and the smoothing serum does the job.

Asher comes out of the bathroom fully dressed in a navy linen short-sleeved shirt, white shorts, and trainers. The tattoos peak out from the edge of the sleeve hem. I want to ask to see it properly because I didn't get the chance earlier, but he speaks first.

"Are you ready? We need to go. Mak has been messaging me."

"Sure. Let me grab my shoes." I sit on the edge of the bed and slip my feet into my trainers. Best to wear them for a walking tour rather than sandals. Then I sling my purse across my shoulders. "Ready."

He steps up to me, and the butterflies return in my stomach. I forget my earlier doubt as he stares into my eyes.

"You look beautiful." He kisses my cheek.

My heart races as I reply. "Thank you. You look nice, too."

He grins as he lifts his head and winks at me. "Come on."

He grabs his bag, and we head downstairs. He flashes his hotel card at the valet, and they bring him a buggy. We drive to the accommodation where he leaves his bag. Then we rush to the restaurant.

By the looks of it, all his young cousins and friends are there, including Mak and Zafe. Then I get introduced to Inna and Ranti as well as younger people. I remember Yomi and Nike because they are teenagers. But I forget the names of the children.

The tour guides arrive, and we head out in three groups because we're too large for one group. In our group are me, Asher, Yomi, and Pearl who is ten years old. Her twin sister Megan is in Zafe's group.

The trip is amazing and inspirational. We walk through the historic narrow streets of the old town displaying distinctive architecture. We visit the old fort, the former sultan's palace renamed the people's palace. We have a sober moment at the old slave market which now has a church built into it.

We stop for lunch at one of the restaurants, and it's nice to be with this lovely family as they banter and joke. People stop and talk to us and ask where we're from and we chorus, 'We're Nigerians' and everyone laughs.

The older women, Ranti and Inna, are polite and friendly to me. But I can sense they are keeping me at arm's length. I can't pinpoint it exactly, and maybe it's just my overactive writer brain imagining things that are not there. Or maybe they know my identity and they've seen the video of my disastrous proposal to Owen.

After lunch, we continue the journey, visiting some gardens and nature reserves. We stop at the market and pick up some souvenirs. Then we visit the town square which is the site of historic protests and political speeches.

Through it all, Asher is the perfect gentleman to me and big brother to Pearl and Yomi. He never lets Pearl stray out of sight and allows her to stop and rest when she becomes tired. He holds my hand, only letting go for brief moments when necessary. He checks I'm okay. Neither one of us is very chatty. We listen to the tour guide as he explains the history of the various sites.

When we make it back to the resort, it's late afternoon. The elder Essiens are on the beach loungers under the canopies. The younger ones rush to greet their parents.

"Let me introduce you," Asher says as he walks towards them.

"No." I stop. My earlier niggle returns, and I feel uncomfortable about staying on. I don't want to face the stern disapproval of Bro Kola or anyone else. I don't need the humiliation of their pity because Owen rejected me.

"What?"

He looks shocked, and I can't blame him. After the pleasant day we've had, I don't want to ruin it by causing any wahala between him and his family.

"I'm going back to my room. It's been a wonderful day, but I'm tired. I need to go and nap." I chicken out of telling him the true reason I'm running.

"Okay, I'll come with you. Just—"

"Asher!" someone calls him, and we turn towards the canopies. The rest of this family is already gathered there. They are looking in our direction, and one of them is waving. "Asher!"

It's Zafe.

"I'm coming," Asher shouts back before turning to me. "Just give me a few minutes to greet them, and I'll walk you back."

"No. There's no need. It'll look somehow if I stand here while you greet them. I'll just go now."

"Fair enough. Okay. Go and take a nap and then meet me at the sports bar this evening for the game." He smiles. "Can I have your phone number?"

He pulls out his phone, and I dictate my number as he types it in. Then my phone starts buzzing in my shoulder bag.

"Now, you have my number. I'll see you tonight." He kisses my cheek.

My face tingles as I turn and walk away. It takes a lot of willpower to leave a man who has shown me nothing but kindness and understanding. When I get to my room, I can't rest. It's as if I'm losing a part of me.

I watch the clock as the sun goes down and the time for today's match draws closer. Yet, I don't leave my room. I can't. I can't face seeing Asher again. I can't go through the heartache of losing him, even though my heart is aching.

Soon, my phone starts buzzing. I look at it, and it's Asher's number. I don't answer it. It cuts off and starts ringing again. When I don't answer it a second time, a text message comes through.

**Where are you? The game is starting now.**

I rub my face and pace the room as I debate what to tell him. Then I settle on the truth. I grab the phone and type.

*I'm not coming to the sports bar tonight.*

**Why? Are you okay? Did something happen?**

*Nothing happened. I just can't see you anymore.*

**Why? I'm coming to your room.**

*No.*

There is no response from him, and a few minutes later, there's a knock on my door.

"Vivi, it's me," I hear his muffled voice through the solid slab of wood.

My heart races, and I fight the urge to race across the room and open the door. Instead, I send a message.

*I told you not to come here.*

**Please open the door.**

*I can't. This thing between us won't work.*

**I care about you.**

*I know. That's the problem.*

**What are you saying? You spent last night with me and most of today.**

*I wanted a holiday fling.*

**Damn. You really know how to cut to the bone.**

*I'm sorry.*

**Nah. Don't apologise. It hurts but at least you're honest.**

My chest constricts. I hate that I've hurt him. I don't know what to say to that. He's as understanding as ever.

**So am I ever going to see you again?**

*Get your team into the Premier League and maybe I'll get to interview you.*

**That's a deal.**

I smile and type.

*The past 24hrs with you have been amazing for me.*

**For me too.**

"Goodbye, Vivi," he says aloud through the door. I can hear the forlorn longing in his voice.

"Bye, Asher," I reply as my voice chokes, and tears well up.

Then his footsteps recede, and he's gone.

Asher

When you have a dream, you should work hard to make it happen. I've always believed this to be true, and it has been my motto.

When I was a child and the teacher asked me what I wanted to do when I grew up, I said I wanted to be a professional football player. Of course, many other children in my school and in schools all over the world wanted to become footballers. But only a few make it this far.

My parents recognised my zeal and actively worked towards making my dreams come true. We had to move home several times while they tried to get me into the right football academy. Although many people said I had talent, I stayed humble and determined. I worked hard to improve my skills.

And that same determination drives me now as I push through the physio training regime to build my body back into shape. I push my body through the series of challenges set by the trainer. I need to rebuild my stamina and strength. Despite my healed injury, my fitness hasn't returned to its peak.

The medics cleared me for training, but I still have to pass the fitness test before I can return to the football field.

It's even more important that I get back on the field because my team is suffering. It doesn't look like we're going to make the automatic qualification spots into the Premier League. However, we still have a chance in the playoffs, and I'm determined to be part of the squad for those games.

So, I'm pushing my body hard. Not only for the ultimate prize of playing in the top EFL league. But also because of her.

Vivi.

I remember our chat the last day I saw her.

***So, am I ever going to see you again?***

*Get your team into the Premier League and maybe I'll get to interview you.*

***That's a deal.***

Hope flares within me.

Viva City Panthers will get into the Premier League.

And I will see Vivi again.

Because that woman walked into my life and rocked my soul for twenty-four hours. Probably the best twenty-hours of my life. I've had amazing moments both on and off the pitch. But the weekend in Zanzibar a month ago is right up there with the most memorable times.

Even if I never see her again, I will never forget her.

They say when life gives you lemons, make lemonade.

Well, I'm squeezing every juicy pulp out of those lemons and adding sugar and spice to give it some kick. That's me.

It's been a month since I returned from the holiday in Zanzibar, since that fateful night and day with Asher, and I'm in the studio working. I had an amazing time over there, and thoughts of Asher are never far from my mind. Sometimes, I think our encounter was fantasy, a figment of my imagination.

But this is reality, and life goes on.

We've just finished doing a recording with a guest—Tisha Bamidele who is a friend and footballer, and her team is still in the Women's FA Cup. It was wonderful to have her in the studio and chat about the upcoming games to round off the season both in the Women's and Men's sports.

She's left already, and I'm with Dave, my co-host, as we work through some of the edits. He handles most of the technical side of the production. We could go home to work on the edits. But this is a good place to listen to the podcast again because of the acoustics. We have a soundproof booth that we use, which is part of a former radio station. It has been remodelled, furnished, and hired out to podcasters. It comes with video and audio recording equipment. We rent it for a few hours a week.

The buzzer for the main door goes off.

"Can you get that," Dave says, headset partially off as he fiddles with the controls on the mixer.

"Sure." I walk to the door.

I wasn't expecting anyone, but sometimes, we order lunch in while we work. So, I assume Dave had done so at some point and it's the delivery person.

"Who is it?" I speak into the small mic attached to the comms panel on the wall.

"It's Owen."

"Owen?" Shock freezes my heart. "What are you doing here?" I ask without thinking.

I haven't spoken to him for two months. His number is still blocked although I know he's been trying to contact me through other people.

"I'm here to see Dave," he replies.

Of course. Dave is his friend. But why didn't my colleague tell me Owen was coming here today? My anger rises as I buzz Owen in and stomp back into the recording studio.

"Why didn't you tell me Owen was coming here today?" I shout at Dave who is still at the mixer.

He looks at me with a frown on his face and lowers the headset. "Owen is here? I didn't know he was coming."

He looks perplexed, as if he didn't know, as his friend walks in behind me. "Mate, you didn't say you were going to pop in."

"Nah, I know we said later, but something came up," Owen replies.

I step out of the way as they embrace and walk to grab my tote and things. For a moment, I thought Owen came here to see me in the guise of seeing his friend. It turns out I'm fooling myself again. I don't even want to look at him. Nausea rolls through me. I gave almost two years of my life to him, and he can't even grovel to win me back. I thought we were tight…

I can't be here. I shove my laptop into the bag and sidestep them as I head to the door.

"Babe, hold up." Owen intercepts me.

"Get out of my way," I snap.

"Don't be like this. Truth is, I came here to see you."

"Me? Why?" I narrow my eyes. He better not come up with a lame excuse.

"Because of this." He reaches into the pocket of his stylish V-neck sweatshirt and trousers combo. This is his standard casual look. He pulls out a small box.

My heart starts racing, and I feel a little dizzy. "That's not what I think it is?"

He smiles as he opens the box, and I see the diamond on platinum engagement ring.

I shake my head as I stumble back.

"Why are you doing this?" I can't help asking because this man rejected my proposal two months ago, and now, he's flashing an engagement ring at me.

"Viv, listen."

"No, you listen," I snap. I hate this shortened form of my name. He used to call me that as a tease, but I'm not in the mood for it. "Don't you dare call me Viv. Your mother calls me Viv and I barely tolerate it. My name is Vivi or Vivian. Full stop."

"Okay. I'm sorry, Vivi." He sounds surly. He's not usually apologetic, so it's pleasing to hear it from him. He really must want me back. "I know I messed up. Mega-ly. I thought I wasn't ready to be engaged to anyone. And you know when you surprised me with the proposal, I just wasn't ready."

"But you're ready now?" I ask in disbelief. This can't be happening.

"I am. The past two months have been difficult, and I missed you. I realise that I need you back in my life. And if being engaged is how we can be together, then let's do it."

"You're serious. You want to marry me."

I sound sceptical, and I am. I clutch my bag to my chest in a protective posture. I don't know

119

if I can trust Owen again although I've missed the times we were together.

"Yes, if that's what it takes to be with you," he replies.

Maybe he wasn't ready to get married. Maybe we could be together without marriage. There are many people who have long-lasting relationships and are not married. I'd read recently about an actress and her long-term partner who was in a rock band. They'd been engaged, split up, and then got back together. They've been together for a decade and not married. So, marriage isn't for everyone.

But here Owen is, willing to change his stance for me.

Still, even if I forgive him, I can't forget his behaviour or the humiliation I experienced. And I'm not about to let it slide. Yes, I can be petty as fuck.

So, I place my bag on the side table and grab my phone. I tap the camera button and start recording, but I don't raise it. "So, is this a proposal?"

"Yes, it is." He grins and comes forward as if all is forgiven.

I raise my palm to stop him. "Hold up there. If you're going to propose to me, you're going to do it properly."

"What do you mean?"

"D'uh. I proposed to you with flowers and candles and music and food. And you just show up like this—" I wave him up and down "—without even making an effort."

"Uh." He growls in frustration. "I've been trying to contact you for weeks, and you've blocked me everywhere. This was the only time I could manage out because it's end of season and we have nonstop training and matches. You know this."

"I know. But it don't mean you can't make an effort."

"So, what do you want me to do?"

"For starters, get on your knees."

"What?" He looks shocked.

"I'm not accepting your proposal if you don't kneel."

"You can't be serious." He glances at Dave who just shrugs.

"Mate, she knelt for you when she proposed. It's only fair that you do the same," Dave says.

The man is being my wingman right now. I'll thank him later.

"You heard him. Otherwise, I'm going." I move to grab my bag.

"Okay." He raises his hand in surrender. Then he lowers his body on one knee.

I raise my phone.

"Are you recording this?" He frowns.

"You betcha."

The world is going to see him on his knees just like they saw me on mine two months ago. Because no one would believe he actually proposed to me after the last debacle without proof. The kind of insults I got online with people calling me desperate because I proposed to him. Nah, I'm still not over it.

The corners of his lips are tight. I know he's not happy on his knees. He's not a man used to being on his knees. But he smiles through it and raises the black velvet jewellery box. This just proves to me how much he wants me.

"Vivi, you know I love you. Please do me the honour of being my wife."

My heart is racing with excitement because Owen is on his knees asking me to be his wife. Yet, I'm a little disappointed the setting is unromantic and he has only done it in two sentences.

I bet Asher Uzodimma would produce better, more significant ways to propose to his future wife. He wrote me a poem on our first meeting, and we slept under the stars.

Now, I'm in a boring studio with nothing exciting except Owen and a ring while his friend looks on. There is no music, no atmosphere. No magic.

His smile is slowly fading as I take a long time to respond. "Vivi, say something. Is it a yes?"

"It's a maybe." I grab my bag and hurry towards the door. "I'll think about it."

# 10

## Vivi

My phone blows up on the way home with messages, and I ignore them. I'm not ready to face queries especially if they are about Owen's proposal.

I should be happy he proposed. That he apologised to me about his behaviour the last time I saw him two months ago.

But I'm not.

I don't know why.

We've dated for close to two years, but it's like I'm suddenly examining everything he does with new lenses. With Asher-tinted lenses, if I'm honest.

Because why didn't I accept Owen's proposal? Why was I comparing it to what I assumed Asher would do in this situation?

I know Owen isn't big on grand gestures. When I met him for the first time at a party and he approached me, of course I was in awe because he's a football player. When he asked for my number, I gave it to him because he was witty and persistent. When he asked me out on a date, I resisted because he had a reputation as a player and I didn't want to be another notch on his bed post. We exchanged messages for a while before I finally agreed to go on a date with him. Even then, it wasn't until our third date that we had sex. And we've been together since.

I was enthused about being the woman who changed his playboy ways. The one he chose as his exclusive. Our love for football and Duke Park Rangers drew us closer. I fell for him, his wit, his skill on the field. On my birthday, he bought me a necklace and took me out to dinner. In the summer, we went to Greece for a holiday together, and I met his parents.

I know what he likes and doesn't like. I know his flaws. Like his ego which sometimes means he's not communicating well with his team mates on the pitch because whenever the ball is passed to him, he feels he should score. Or his dark moods when DPR lose a game.

His flaws make him human, and I understand it. No one is perfect.

Certainly not me.

So, on paper, we're a good match.

Hence my reason for wanting a future with him. Being with him made me happy.

Or so I thought. Until I went to Zanzibar and met a man who blew all my interactions with Owen out of the water.

Twenty-four hours with Asher, and I'm questioning my future with Owen.

I want more. I want grand gestures and magical moments. I want to feel butterflies in my stomach when I receive a proposal. I want to feel excitement and ecstatic giddiness with joy.

And Owen's proposal today just didn't cut it.

At the very least, he should have taken the hint from my proposal to him and the way I set it up. That should have told him what I like.

Unfortunately, this seems to be the thing with Owen. I think he doesn't notice things about me unless it suits him.

Or maybe I'm blowing things out of proportion.

Drama queen me.

But perhaps I'm right to want more.

Owen was my first serious boyfriend. I didn't date when I was younger.

As a teenager, I played sports and hung out with boys talking sports. But I never got intimate with them in that way. I was a tomboy and wore clothes that made me appear androgynous. It wasn't really until my mid-twenties that I became confident about my body and appearance as a woman.

Then Owen showed up, and I fell in love with him.

When I get home, Temi is waiting. We share a two-bed-flat in a new-build because neither of us is as rich as footballers. She must have heard me turning the key in the lock because she is standing in the small hallway outside the kitchen.

"Are you okay?" she asks straightaway.

"Not really," I reply as I walk past her into the kitchen.

She follows me. "Owen called me."

"Yeah... and?" I dump my tote on the counter and open the fridge.

"And he said he proposed to you."

"And?"

I grab a bottle of water and reach into the overhead cupboard for a glass. The modern minimalist kitchen units have flat-panel doors crafted from high-quality plywood and finished with Aegean-blue wood veneer. There's an island counter with two tall white wooden stools. The rest of the flat is refurbished to a high standard.

"And you tell me?" She leans on the panel doors of the tall fridge-freezer.

I sigh and pour myself a cold drink. Then I gulp it down while she waits for my response.

"And I said maybe." I take my bag and head to my room.

"You said maybe. Why? I thought you want to marry Owen."

"I did." I place the bag on my bedside table, sit on the bed, and start taking my boots off.

"You did? Vivi, what's going on." She walks in and sits on the bed beside me, watching me with confusion in her gaze.

I sigh heavily again and lower my head. "I just ... I feel differently now. I want more."

"More what?" Her face screws up even more. "I don't understand."

"I'll show you."

I'm not sure I can verbally explain what I'm trying to articulate so I pull my phone from my bag, unlock the screen, and dig out the recording from Owen's proposal and play it for her.

She sits quietly and watches it until the end. "Well…"

"Well, exactly. That's the most boring, unimaginative proposal ever."

"Yes, it is, by your standards. You like the fantastical and the bold and the beautiful."

"Exactly. Anyone who knows me knows what I like. But he didn't make any effort. Didn't even bring flowers with the proposal."

"Yeah, but this is Owen, innit. We know he's not very imaginative. He's never going to compile a playlist for you or write you poems."

"But someone did," I blurt out and regret it immediately as Temi's eyes widen.

"Wait, what? Someone wrote you a poem. Who?" she asks, not missing a beat.

I shift in discomfort because I hid this from her for a reason. "It's no one."

"Come on, cuz. You can't be hiding things from me. Spill already."

"If I tell you, you can't tell anyone else," I insist.

"Ah ah. Why are you like this? I'm not a gossip," she says in a teasing tone, mimicking a character off a Black British sitcom.

"I'm serious, Temi. I don't want this getting out for several reasons."

"Okay," she says in a serious tone. "I cross my heart. Tell me."

"I met someone while I was in Zanzibar," I start.

"Okay?" She waves her hand, urging me on.

"You know I told you about this Nigerian family that shut down half the resort."

"Yes, somebody's birthday party, and you mentioned you met some footballers who play in Italy."

"Yes. What I didn't mention was that one of the footballers plays in England. In the Championship."

"Oh." She sits up. "Who is it?"

"Asher Uzodimma," I blurt out.

She tilts her head sideways and looks up at the ceiling briefly as she thinks about the name. I see the moment it clicks because her eyes widen and she looks at me as if I have two heads.

"Asher Uzodimma, the one that plays for …" she trails off.

"Viva City Panthers," I finish off.

"Rara. No. Mba nu." She goes from Yoruba to English to Igbo like the multi-tribal woman she is. "This is not true."

Annoyed, I get off the bed and start walking away.

"Where are you going?" she asks, and I round on her.

"This is why I didn't tell you anything when I returned from Zanzibar. I knew you would react like this."

"I'm sorry, but you haven't really told me anything." She looks apologetic, and I calm down somewhat.

I return to the bed. "I met Asher at the sports bar I told you about. He bought me a drink and told Faraji the bartender to bring it to me. I was watching a game so I didn't talk to Asher. But after the game when I looked at where he was sitting, he wasn't there anymore. I asked Faraji about him, and the barman pulled a sheet of paper out of his pocket. Asher had written me a note asking me to meet him the next day. But it wasn't an ordinary note. Hold on."

I go to the bedside table and open the top drawer. Then I pull out my journal. I open it to the right page and take out the sheet before passing it to Temi.

She unwraps and reads it. "Wow. Asher wrote this to you."

"Yes."

"It's lovely."

"I know." I sit beside her. "When I read it, it was as if he shone a light on a part of me that was in the shadows. I went looking for him that night. I knew he was going to be at the party because it was his uncle's party. So, I gate-crashed it pretending I was his Plus One and I was nearly kicked out. But Asher saved me twice. He didn't have to."

"Probably because he wanted to get in your knickers."

"That's the thing. I spent all night with him, and we didn't have sex. We didn't even French kiss."

"What? Maybe he's gay."

"No, Asher is not gay. I mean, he could be bi or pan. But he's definitely into women." I don't bother explaining. Bro Kola's comment about Asher and street girls replay in my mind.

"So, nothing happened between you and Asher?"

"Nothing sexual happened. However, it was the most romantic twenty-four hours of my life."

"Really?"

"Yes."

"So now, you don't want to marry Owen because of Asher. Are you still seeing him?"

"No. I haven't seen him since before I left Zanzibar. But that's not the point. The point is that spending the time with Asher has made me want more from my relationships. Asher set the standard. And at the moment, Owen is lagging behind."

"Hang on. You only spent twenty-four hours with this man, and you're using him as a standard. You know it was a holiday, and the man was probably on his best behaviour."

"Nah. You won't understand unless you were there. He wasn't pretending or even trying too hard. I think he was genuinely being himself. Anyway, I'm saying all this to say that I still care about Owen. I just wish he would be more romantic. More considerate. Is that too much to ask?"

"No—"

My buzzing phone interrupts our conversation, and I look at the caller ID. It's my agent, Emily. She's gotten me gigs from modelling fashion wear for online retailers to radio presenting.

"Emily, hi," I answer the call, wondering what gig she has lined up for me next.

"Oh, good, I caught you this time, Vivi. How are you?"

"I'm good. And you?"

"I'm even better. I have some good news for you. I called you earlier, but it went to voicemail."

"Oh. It must have been when I was on The Tube on my way home. What's up?"

"So, there's this new TV programme for a major streaming service. They're looking for young celebrity couples to participate, and I thought you'd be a good fit. This would be a huge boost for your profile because you could be in front of millions of viewers not just in the UK but across the world."

My pulse accelerates. "This sounds very interesting. But did you say couples?"

"Yes. It's a *Wife Swap* meets *Real Housewives* type format with couples. How are things going between you and Owen?"

It seems I can't get away from Owen.

"You know we had a problem a while back," I say.

"That's a shame. Is there no way you two can get back together? I think the two of you will be explosive on camera. The TV producers will love you."

She isn't wrong. I always thought Owen and I make a hot couple. And I've always wanted to do a TV show to boost my profile. This sounds like a once in a lifetime opportunity. And Owen would love it, too. Could I blow it all because I was comparing Owen to Asher? I have the future to think of. My future. And it doesn't involve Asher Uzodimma.

"Well, Owen proposed to me today," I say finally.

"That's wonderful. Congratulations to both of you. Should I take it that I should put you down for the show?"

"Yes."

"Great. This is going to be wonderful for both of you. You'll see. Let me get the ball rolling for you. I'll be in touch."

"Thank you, Emily."

"Bye, Vivi."

I end the call.

"What was that?" Temi asks.

"Just a minute," I reply as I open the blocked numbers list on my phone and unblock Owen's number. I guess my thinking time is over and the answer has been given to me.

I send him a message.

*My answer is yes to the proposal. I will marry you.*

# Asher

Some of my fondest memories involves standing in line at an event waiting for my ball or jersey to be signed by one of my footballing heroes. Now here I am walking along a wall of people calling out my name, asking for an autograph.

I'm attending a charity event organised by Life Sports, a local NGO, and the Viva City

Borough Council. It's an annual event that commemorates the end of the EFL season.

But our season is not over yet because we've ended up in third place on the Championship table, which means we qualify for a place in the playoffs. So, we still have a chance to get to the Premier League next season.

I'm excited although I returned to the team too late in the season to get us to the top spot. I was able to score crucial goals in the last two games which kept us in the running for the playoffs. We've come this far, and I'm hoping we'll go the distance into the Premier League.

Still, I can't dull the rush of adrenaline. It's the first time Viva City Panther has reached the playoffs since we made it into the penultimate division of the English Football League. My entire life, I have been working for this big moment.

The chant of my name from the crowd, the lights ricocheting off flashing cameras from the reporters, I soak it all up. I am so ready for the next stage of my life. I'm on the edge of stardom, I can feel it. I want to savour it.

I stop and sign autographs, shake hands and ruffle the hair of smiling children on the other side of the hip-high barricades. A reporter shoves a microphone in my face, and I'm pelted with questions. I answer them with a smile and even crack some jokes. I'm buzzed because I'm back in the squad, back playing the game I love. Although I missed out being the Championship Player of the Year for the second year running because I missed a quarter of the season, there's still a chance to achieve my dreams.

The only thing—person—missing is Vivi.

She's been on my mind every single day. It's like she's with me, challenging me, motivating me with her words.

*Make it to the Premier League and maybe I'll interview you.*

It's like a destiny written in the stars, and I believe it will come to pass.

From the corner of my eye, I see the rest of my teammates walking into the hall. I put my arm around my mother in a protective manner and guide her through the crowd to the entrance.

I always take my mum to the big events because she was always there for me with the little ones. She was there for every football practice when I was little. We moved houses several times while my parents were trying to find me the right football academy. She came to my games when I started playing in the junior and senior teams. She sacrificed so much of her time, money, and effort for me.

So, whenever there's a big occasion within the sporting world and I'm invited, I take her along. She's always excited about showing up because she knows how far I've come. While my teammates might bring their spouses, I'm not ashamed to show up with my mother. She is my anchor and my comfort.

Not matter what changes happened in my life or even when I spiralled out of control as a teenager, she never gave up on me. Sure, she shipped me off to go and stay with my cousins in Nigeria because she thought I might fall into gangs in the UK. But she still believed in me. She was determined I would have the best opportunities available to me.

Don't get me wrong. My dad encourages me, too. But he has his hands full in charge of his flock at Kingdom Come Tabernacle as General Overseer. He never fully understood my obsession with football, but he didn't stop me from pursuing my dreams. He just wasn't the father standing out in the freezing rain watching his son kick the ball in the mud.

Then again, I'm the last child of five, and I have an older brother, Jeremiah, who is more or less following in my father's footsteps. My three sisters, Hannah, Rebecca, and Esther, used to tease me and call me Mummy's Handbag when I was little because I used to hang onto her a lot.

Now, although I'm taller than her by about a foot, I'm still happy to be Mummy's Boy.

In the hall, we're ushered to our table. I get her seated first before I settle in mine. We're offered refreshments and nibbles. On the stage, there are speeches by the mayor and other dignitaries, followed by a five-course meal. Afterwards is an auction of several items donated by the two football clubs in the area—Viva City Panthers and Duke Park Rangers. The items sell very quickly and expensively, but it's all in the aid of the local charities. It's also an opportunity for corporate networking as there are business and potential corporate sponsors here, too.

Once the auctions ends, the DJ takes over and plays music. Those who want to dance use the floor. I mingle and introduce my mother to everyone I chat with. Of course, she's in her African multi-print dress with a silk wrap draped over her shoulders. We're in a room mostly full of Caucasians in beige and cool pastels. So, my mother stands out. She is bold and beautiful. Just like another woman I met recently...

I see a flash of colour—fuchsia—and turn instinctively towards it. But I lose it in the crowd.

My heart is racing, my skin hot. Could it be her? Vivi. Is she here?

"Mum, I think I spotted someone I need to speak to. Do you mind?"

"No. It's okay. I need to use the ladies, anyway. I'll meet you back at the table."

"Okay."

I direct her towards the signs for the ladies and keep glancing around. But I can't see anyone wearing the bright purple/red colour I spotted earlier. Then I head down the corridor leading to the foyer, thinking she might have gone outside.

My heart stops as I halt. Then it slams into my chest.

A woman stands in the foyer talking on her phone. Her back is to me, but I recognise her figure, her voice.

Vivi is here. I don't know how it's possible. I mean, I know she lives in London and she works as a sportswriter. But to be here at this very moment feels like serendipity. Like destiny.

My senses heighten, and my vision clarifies. I was buzzing when I arrived. But now, it feels like I've been struck by lightning and energy surges through me. It transports me to that first night I saw her in the sports bar. I zoom in on her.

She's in an off-shoulder, ruffle collar, boho maxi dress that shows off the glowing brown skin of her shoulders and arms and skims her curves. It's sexy without being vulgar. Her strappy stilettoes match her purse tucked under her arm.

Her hair is different. In Zanzibar, her hair had loose curls and streaks of colour. This looks too dark, long and straight and almost to her butt. Perhaps a wig or weave, just like my sisters wear sometimes.

Her voice is a melody that draws me closer, and I can't resist the pull. I walk past the people around me as if they are obstacles and challenges I must conquer to reach my goal—Vivi. Adrenaline charges over me. I'm on the field in a crucial match, and I'm running toward the goal line to score before the final whistle.

As if she senses me, she swivels, and I know I'm not dreaming because her face lights up with a beautiful smile. Warmth and ecstasy spread through me. I want to touch her smooth skin, to kiss her full lips a shade darker than her dress. Her irises are a mesmerising bronze. There are layers of colours on her eyelids and cheeks, contouring her face. It's more makeup than she had on the island.

But I recognise the woman underneath. I remember the natural tone of her skin first thing in the morning. The softness of her curves against me. Every cell in my body wants to be connected to her.

"My Lady in Fuchsia," I whisper huskily as if I've just sprinted to her, remembering the note I wrote her over a month ago.

"I have to go now," she says to whoever is on the line and lowers her phone. "Asher."

The sound of my name from her lips is breathy and inviting. I almost forget where I am as I step closer.

"It's good to see you." She doesn't know how much. I can barely control my joy at seeing her. I know I'm grinning like a fool. "You look amazing."

I can't hide the awe in my voice. I don't want to hide it. I want her to know exactly how she makes me feel.

"Thank you." She tilts her head shyly. "You, too."

I'm wearing a two-piece black linen tunic and trouser set with gold embroidered seams. I know I look good, but I'm nowhere as beautiful as her. Standing this close to her, I can smell her intoxicating perfume, and I want to immerse myself in it.

"So how have you been? Are you working tonight, or is this pleasure?" I ask.

"I'm good, thanks. Tonight is a bit of both." She shifts uncomfortably and avoids my gaze, and I sense something is wrong. I want to ask, but she continues. "I saw your last two games. Well done for getting your team into the playoffs."

"Thank you. It was a tough road getting here. But you motivated me."

"Me?"

"Yes. Have you forgotten? You promised to interview me when my team makes it into the Premier League."

"Oh, I remember that. You're going to have to work really hard at the playoffs."

"I'm ready." I grin and spot someone walking along the corridor. "By the way, I want to introduce you to my mother."

"I'm not sure that's a good idea."

"Listen, there's no need to be scared. My mum is the best. I promise." I hurry down the corridor. "Mum!" I call out.

She turns and smiles. "I wondered where you were. Can we go home now?"

"Of course. But I want to introduce you to a good friend." I turn as Vivi approaches. "This is Vivi."

"Vivi? That same Vivi, okwa ya?" my mum says with a smile.

"Yes," I reply and smile at Vivi.

"Good evening, ma," Vivi says, dipping at the knees briefly.

"Good evening, my dear." My mum embraces her from the side. "It's nice to meet you. My son said really nice things about you."

Vivi rubs her neck as she glances at me in surprise. "Mrs Uzodimma, I didn't do much."

"Even if it was a little thing you did, it mattered to him. I'm grateful. Thank you."

"Vivi! There you are," a male voice calls out.

I turn, coming face to face with Owen Price, my nemesis.

"Owen." Vivi turns, too. "I was just saying hello to Asher Uzodimma and his mother." She turns back to face us, her smile gone. "Mrs Uzodimma, this is Owen Price. He plays for Duke's Park Rangers."

"Yes, it's nice to meet you, Mrs Yuzodeema." He wraps a possessive arm around Vivi's waist as he speaks and then looks up at me with a smirk as if he knows I'm interested in her and he's staking his claim. "I'm Vivi's fiancé."

My stomach congeals. Is this true? Vivi is engaged to Owen Price?

I look at her face, but she avoids my gaze. Oh, shit. He moves her left hand which was tucked behind her back, and I see the glittering ring. She was trying to hide it from me.

I'm speechless and frozen. Because in all my imaginings, I didn't picture her as belonging to my mortal enemy. Oh, Vivi, why? Owen Price, of all people.

"It's nice meeting you," my mum says politely and nudges me.

"Good night," I say curtly and move into action, steering my mother towards the exit.

Outside, the huge crowds have diminished, although there are a few stragglers. Mum doesn't say anything as we walk across the car park to where I left the vehicle. I open the door, settle her in before going around to the driver's side of the two-door S-Class coupe AMG. I press the ignition and drive out of the car park, heading towards my parents' house.

"She is the one, isn't she?" Mum asks in the quiet car.

I don't need to ask what she means because she knows what Vivi means to me just by the way I've spoken about her. I've never spoken about any other woman in the same way to my mother.

I swallow the lump in throat, trying to not succumb to the despair hovering around me. I don't want to fall back into depression.

"Yes. She is the one." I force the words out.

"Listen to me. This is just another passing trial. You will overcome. The night is darkest before dawn. Do not despair. This too shall pass."

"Amen," I affirm.

She goes on and recites the prayer from Psalm 91 from memory over me. Afterwards, I have the Gospel playlist blasting from the speakers.

Even after I drop her off, I don't change the music. It lifts my spirits, and by the time I get home, I'm back in a good place.

# 12

"Why are you like this?" I say in a rush, wriggling out of Owen's grabby hands as soon as Asher and his mother are out of sight.

Seeing Asher again raised a swell of emotions swirling inside me. Awe, desire, confliction, longing, regret. He is as tall, dark, and handsome as I remember him. Still as charming and polite, respectful and considerate. The woman was dignified and graceful. It's easy to see why Asher is the way he is and where he got it from.

Swivelling to face my fiancé, I'm reminded he is almost an opposite of Asher. Don't get me wrong, Asher is not a choir boy. I've done some research on him, and his past is not exactly squeaky clean. I know why I was attracted to him.

They both have bad boy swagger. But while Asher seems to know when to turn the cockiness into charm and consideration, Owen's arrogance knows no bounds. He just doesn't know when to stop or doesn't care.

"What did I do?" He shrugs lazily. He's wearing a smirk of satisfaction that says he knows exactly what he's doing. Exactly what he did.

"Why were you groping me in front of Asher's mother? Don't you know it's disrespectful to me? To Mrs Uzodimma," I say in a harsh whisper, conscious we're in a public venue and there will be eavesdroppers.

I don't even want to think about how his display made Asher feel after he was so nice to introduce me to his mother. From their quick exit, I will assume Asher is hurt. I didn't mean to hurt him. In fact, although I knew he would be here today, I thought I could avoid him until the event ended. But he discovered me anyway.

Owen tugs me into a corner, away from prying eyes. "What do you mean, disrespectful? I'm your fiancé. I'm allowed to touch you in public."

"Not like that. You're not entitled to my body because we're engaged," I snap.

This is a bone of contention between us because I've refused to have sex with him since we got back together. He's not happy about it one bit. But tough. I know he fucked around during our break-up, and I'm not sure he's still not at it with others. I'm engaged to him, but I don't trust him.

"Are you fucking kidding me?" he barks.

The smell of booze from his breath catches me off-guard. The football season is over, but not for Duke's Park Rangers who are in the Championship playoffs competing for a place in the Premier League next season. So, he isn't allowed alcohol until the playoffs are over. I didn't see him with alcohol while we were in the banquet hall. Perhaps he drank some after I left to make a phone call.

"Owen, have you been drinking?" I ask, changing the topic as I angle my body away so I don't get drunk from his breath.

He averts his gaze and shifts from one foot to the other. "How is it your business?"

"It's my business because we came in your car. And I'm not letting you drive if you're drunk."

"Do I look fucking drunk to you?" he says defensively, talking too fast, and I narrow my eyes at him.

"That's not even the point. You have football training tomorrow. The coach will bench you if you're not fit for the first round of playoffs."

"Coach is not stupid enough to bench the best player in the team," he says arrogantly.

"The way you are right now, you're the weakest fucking link."

As soon as I say it, I regret it. But this man just brings out the worst in me sometimes.

"What did you just say to me?" he says in a low, menacing voice.

"I didn't mean that." I swallow. "I'm just frustrated. We finished below the Loons in the table so we need to fucking win our playoff matches."

"And you don't think I can do it?" His nostrils flare, and he looms closer, making me back up against the wall. "Do you think that fucking Asher is a better player than me?"

"No. That's not what I meant. I shouldn't have said that."

My mouth runs away with itself sometimes. I really shouldn't have said that to him.

Owen is not someone I can tease in such a manner, and saying it in anger only means he will use it against me.

"So how do you know him?" He's still in my face, glaring down at me.

"I met him before, okay," My tone is sharp, hiding my guilt. Although why I feel guilt, I don't know. Nothing happened between me and Asher.

I mean, sure, I'm attracted to him. And seeing him again resurrected those feelings. But we can't be together. One, I'm engaged to someone else. Two, Asher is in a rival club.

"Well, you better remember he's a Pantaloon. An opp." He stares at me and then shakes his head as he steps back. "Call Dave to pick you up."

He starts walking away.

"What? Where are you going?" I follow him down the steps to the exit.

"I'm getting away from my nagging fiancée." He laughs derisively before he walks out.

"Wait. What?" I glance around. There are other people in the foyer, but he doesn't seem to care. He's embarrassing me publicly again. They are all staring at me. My cheeks heat from mortification.

I can't stay here so I leave the building as Owen drives out of the carpark in a squeal of tyres. I'm shaking and fuming as I walk to the taxi stand about five minutes away. It's dark and late, but the stand is outside the train station which is on a busy road. My feet are hurting by the time I get into a black cab to take me home.

I can't believe Owen left me at the venue although I wouldn't have wanted to be in the car with him. Not with the way he drove out of the car park.

What is wrong with the man? Why does he behave so erratically?

Bending forward in the car seat, I cover my face with my hands and fight tears.

Ever since we got engaged, we've been working on getting our relationship back on track in preparation for the TV show. But one thing after another keeps going wrong.

Owen's performance on the field has been less than great. In turn, his mood at home has been spiralling. Tonight was a huge example. And it seems he's drinking.

When we started dating, we agreed he wouldn't drink during the football season to help keep his body in top condition. It seems he must have fallen off the wagon at some point when we broke up a few months ago.

Where has he gone to tonight? Hopefully, he's gone to his apartment to sleep it off. I wasn't joking when I mentioned training tomorrow. We need him in top form on the team. Otherwise, we'll struggle through the playoffs.

When the taxi stops outside my flat, I pay the driver and step out. The neighbourhood is quiet as I hurry up the stairs and into the building. Temi is away on a business trip so the flat is dark. I turn on the hallway light and go straight to my bedroom. Then I strip off, take the wig off, and cover my cornrowed hair with a shower cap. I walk into the ensuite and step into the shower enclosure.

The scented soap and cascading water help to wash away the dirt and some of my stress. I come out, dry my body, and change into my PJ set. Then I climb into bed.

I grab my phone from the bedside and start typing a message to Asher. I know I hurt his feelings today, and he doesn't deserve it. The least I can do is apologise.

*I'm sorry about what happened earlier today. I didn't want you to find out about Owen like that.*

I hold the phone in my hand after I send it, but nothing happens for a few minutes. Letting out a sigh, I shift to place the gadget back on the side table when a message flashes. It's from Asher, and I click to read it at once.

*Why didn't you tell me you are engaged?*

*I don't know. I didn't want to hurt you.*

*But you did.*

*I know. I'm sorry. I seem to do that to you a lot.*

*So you were dating him when we were together in Zanzibar.*

*No. I wouldn't do that. Owen and I split up. It's the reason I was in Zanzibar alone.*

*But you're engaged to him now.*

*It's complicated.*

*That seems to be your answer every time. You said the same thing when you dumped me in Zanzibar.*

*But it's true.*

*Is it? Or are you playing it safe because you're afraid to commit to me. You're afraid that I will love you like no one else has ever done. That you will love me in return. Do you think you're better with the devil you know rather than the angel you don't?*

*You're no angel!*

**I'm not. But I'm damned better than that asshole you call a fiancé.**

I don't reply immediately because I can't deny his claim. Asher is a better human than Owen, there is no doubt about it. But I'm not quite ready to explain the full situation yet. Mostly because of the TV deal business. If I didn't have it, I would dump Owen in a flash because he's being too much. But he could also be my ticket to the big leagues, and after two years of nonsense with him, I deserve the best.

My phone pings with a message from Asher.
**Goodnight, Vivi.**
Good night, Asher.

I send back with a forlorn smile. He really is a good person. His handsome face stays on my mind, and my last thought as I fall asleep is that he's right. I'm afraid. But I'm already in love with him.

<u>13</u>

*Vivi*

On Sunday, I'm at my mum's house. Well, I say I'm in my mum's house, but I'm actually physically in Temi's parents' house which is a few doors down in the terraced row of houses. Yes, my mother and her twin sister live next to each other. I guess they didn't want to be separated as adults.

When we were kids, we used to walk in and out of each other's houses. We still do. This was great when I was growing up, especially since I'm an only child, and my father died when I was young. It was nice having cousins to hang with all day and still go home when I needed solitude. As a single parent, my mother worked long hours as a nurse. So I was in Temi's house before school and after school. It's a second home to me.

My uncle and aunt have had their ups and downs and quarrels. There have been separations, and still, they get back together. There's a rumour that Uncle Segun has a mistress and another family. But I've never seen anything.

My mum doesn't discuss such matters with me. On her part, my mum has dated several men. There was a period where there seemed to be a new man every Christmas. But she's mellowed now, although she's only fifty-five. She married young, and I think losing her husband early traumatised her. Plus, she has her sister next door. Why change the family dynamics?

Temi is still away on the work thing and should be back next week. But I don't want to be in the flat by myself. I keep waking up in the middle of the night thinking there's someone in the flat with me.

I haven't felt right all week. Not since the incident with Owen at the fundraising event. He called me to apologise for his behaviour and said the stresses of the season were finally getting to him. I said I understood, but he should take to week to focus on the upcoming match and get his act together. He agreed, and I haven't seen him since.

In my heart, I know I will break up with him at some point. I don't want to rock the boat until the playoffs are over, and I don't want to add to his stress. So, I'm taking one for the team because I want Duke's Park Rangers to qualify for the playoff final.

I messaged him to wish him good luck for today's game.

It's the championship playoff weekend. Both semifinal matches are on today.

Duke's Park Rangers is playing away to Eastborough Rovers and kick off is around midday. Later this afternoon, Viva City Panthers will be at home against Longmead Athletics.

The air is thick with excitement in the whole of the borough. People are wagering that the finals in Wembley in two weeks will be DPR vs VCP.

I can see the Panthers getting through. Asher is back in the squad, and they haven't lost any games to Longmead Athletics in the previous clashes this season.

On the other hand, for the Rangers, Eastborough is a tough opponent unless we have a really good game. Which is why I need Owen playing his A game today.

Instead, I'm in my auntie's house watching it on the big screen TV with Uncle Segun, Temi's dad. Her brother Dele is here, too. The women are over at my mum's house. That's part of the routine.

On Sundays, they go to church at the Anglican service down the road. When they return, they pop into my mum's house to cook and chat. I would pop over here after doing my chores because there's no way my mum would let me just sit and watch footie without contributing to the meal. We'd sit in front of the telly and eat the meal.

Well, everyone else except me.

I don't eat until the game is over.

Today, the meal is done early so I grab a quick bite before the match starts and park my behind on the sofa.

The match kicks off on the telly, and when Owen is listed to play, my body releases its tension. DPR has a fighting chance. But the game is lacklustre from both sides and ends in a nil-nil draw. The only good thing about it is that the return match will be on home turf for DPR.

There is about forty minutes until the VCP game starts. I send Asher a good luck message. He probably won't see it until later. But he'll know I was thinking of him before the match.

I pop over to my mum's. She and my aunt grill me about my engagement to Owen. It's my first time with them since the proposal. Luckily, they seem more interested in planning the imaginary wedding than in any in-depth detail about the state of my relationship with Owen. Hence, I manage to deflect all the questions. I haven't told them about the TV show or about Asher.

They talk about calling the church parish to book a date, whether it will be a spring or summer wedding. Who would be invited. I haven't even talked about any of those things with Owen.

Neither of us seems interested in setting an actual date.

I have no idea if Owen wants a destination wedding or a local church one. Whether he wants a summer or winter one.

Suddenly, the clarity of it dawns on me.

When I proposed to Owen, I did it because it was a Leap Year, and I didn't want to miss the opportunity. Sure, I wanted to be able to say I put a ring on his finger. But it was content for my followers to consume, too.

When he proposed to me, I only agreed because of the TV deal my agent offered. I don't think I would have said yes otherwise.

I don't want to marry Owen. I love the idea of a wedding, but the person I picture as the groom is not Owen.

It's Asher.

Asher! The game. I glance at my phone and see the time. Then I excuse myself and return to my aunt's house to watch the VCP vs Longmead game.

Temi's brother Dele is, interestingly, a VCP supporter. He switched sides as an adult.

When they show the lineup for VCP on screen, and I see Asher's name, my pulse skyrockets. When they show him entering the stadium with the rest of the team, I can barely contain my excitement.

"My boy Asher looks so pumped and ready for this game," Dele says.

"He does," I reply. It feels good to have someone else here supporting VCP so I don't feel like the odd one out. "So, what do you think the scores will be?"

"As long as our back four keep their shit tight, I'm thinking three-nil," he says.

I chuckle. "You're very confident."

"I am. We have fresh legs in the team. Asher Uzodimma is back from injury, and Nonso Chijuka is back from suspension. The team found their form again. Longmead should just concede already. Let's head to Wembley and the final."

He is not wrong. Viva City Panthers seems to have stronger team now than they had at the start of the season.

The game is exciting and ends at three goals to one in VCP's favour. Asher scored two of those goals. I'm so excited when he scores, I'm bouncing off the chair.

"Don't tell me you've switched over to their side," my uncle comments at one point.

"Daddy, can you blame her? See the way the Panthers walked all over this field," Dele says, saving me from replying. "In fact, I predict that VCP will win the Playoff Final."

"Ah." Uncle Segun clutches his chest in a pained dramatic display, shaking his head. "It will be my own son that will betray me."

I burst out laughing. You wonder where I get my penchant for drama, it's from my family.

"Daddy, you better switch sides, too, and save yourself the heart attack when DPR lose," Dele jokes.

I continue giggling, but I can't help feeling as if I should do the same. Switch sides and save myself the heart ache. Because could I possibly be in love with Asher and remain a DPR fan? Could I keep supporting Owen and his team when I've fallen out of love with him?

My reaction to the two games this afternoon is proof of where my loyalties now lie. Even though I don't want to initiate a split from Owen until the end of the playoffs, my heart is not with him nor with DPR. Sure, I want them to do well, but I'm not about to stress myself about it. If DPR plays VCP at the final in Wembley, I know I will be cheering for Asher and his team.

When I get home later that evening, I stash the takeaway boxes of Nigerian food into the freezer. One advantage of going home is that I return with packs of foods from my mum. I especially love her moimoi.

After a shower, I get into bed. Tomorrow is Monday, and I have a busy schedule. For one thing, I need to call my agent and let her know about my change of status. I'm hoping they won't mind who my spouse is as long as I show up with one for the TV show.

This makes me think about Asher. I don't know how he'll feel about being in a reality show.

I know I'm jumping the gun since we're not officially an item.

But I know when I'm single again, he'll ask me out.

I'm sure of it.

He's been straightforward from the first day I met him.

No harm in asking him, though. I grab my phone and send him a text.

*Congratulations on a great win today. Do you have time to talk.*

I've barely clicked send before my phone buzzes. It seems he's been sitting there waiting to talk to me as much as I have wanted to talk to him.

My hand trembles as I answer the call.

"Hey, Asher," I say in a soft voice.

"Hi, Vivi. Thank you for the messages today. I appreciate them." His voice is husky with a tinge of excitement.

"You're welcome. You and the team did an amazing job today."

"I told you we're going all the way to the Premier League," he says confidently.

I laugh. "Yes, you did, and I believe you."

"You do?"

"Yes. You deserve to win the playoffs. You've all worked hard, especially you."

"It means a lot to me to hear you say that."

"Does it?"

"Yes. I've been sitting here since I came home waiting for the buzz to die down, wanting to call you."

"You have? So why didn't you?"

"Because..." he pauses, and it sounds like he's moving. "Because you ended things between us in Zanzibar. Because you're engaged to another man."

I can hear the longing in his voice, and it echoes mine.

"What if I tell you I don't want to end things? What if I told you I'm breaking off the engagement with Owen?"

"Then I'll get in my car and drive over to your place right now, and I'll show you exactly how much I've been wanting you. But..." he trails off for a few seconds.

"But what?" My heart's so racing, and I'm hot and trembling because I want him here.

"But don't give me hypotheticals. You know I've been into you since Zanzibar. I've not hidden it from you. I can't do side tings, you know. I have too much respect for myself. For you. So don't build me up only to shatter my heart. Don't lead me on, Vivi."

"I'm not leading you on. I am breaking things off with Owen. It's just that I don't want to tell him yet because of the playoffs. I don't want to be the reason his head is not in the game. It's not fair to him."

It's not fair to me, but I was the one who accepted this proposal when I shouldn't have. I should have said no right there in the podcast studio.

"Hmmm," Asher murmurs in contemplation. "So, you're breaking it off with Owen, why?"

"Because I don't love him. I don't want to spend the rest of my life with him. He's done some things…"

"What things?" I can hear the sharpness of his tone as if he's ready to take on Owen. "Did he hit you?"

"No. Nothing like that. But he's been threatening, and his mood keeps deteriorating. Can you imagine he left me at the Civic Centre on the night of the fundraising and drove away—"

"He did what?"

"That was after shouting at me in front of other people. I had to walk to the station to get a taxi."

"Nah nah nah. Is he ment? And you're still with him?"

"I told you it's over. I haven't seen him since that night although we've messaged each other. Once the playoffs are over, I'm returning his ring and ending it."

"Look, Vivi. I hear you. But I'm worried. I don't think you really know Owen Price. He's not a bad boy of Championship football for nothing. He's the king of revenge. You know the injury he caused me in February was revenge for me getting him booked during a match from the previous season. He never forgives or forgets. The worse that happens to him on the field is suspension and a fine. But for you, I worry about what he can do to you."

"No. Owen has never been violent towards me. Sure, he loses his temper. But he just walks away. His way of punishing me is to humiliate me in front of other people."

"I don't know, Vivi. But at least you don't live alone. So, you should be alright there. Just be careful when you're out and about."

"My cousin Temi is away, but she'll be back in a few days."

"Are you saying you're in the flat by yourself?"

"Yes, but—"

"I'm coming over now. Text me your address."

"Asher it's not necessary."

"Vivi, if you know nothing about me, know that there's no way I will sleep peacefully knowing you're on Owen's turf. And he can get to you anytime."

The thought of him not getting any sleep gives me pause. "You really don't have to do this."

"I know. But this is who I am. One day, I will tell you the story of my past and why I listen to my instincts. And my instincts say I shouldn't leave you alone."

His words spook me, and I remember the number of nights I've woken up feeling like I wasn't alone since Temi went on her trip.

"Okay. I'll send you my address."

# 14

## Asher

Adrenaline scores through me, and it's a miracle I keep to the speed limit as I drive down the dual carriage towards Vivi's house.

I still can't believe she called me tonight.

Lord knows how many times I've wanted to grab my phone and call her since the debacle of finding out her engagement to Owen Price at the Civic Centre a week ago.

Gosh. Has it only been a week?

From the moment I met Vivi, I knew she was my dream girl, the woman I wanted to spend the rest of my life with. But life isn't always fair, and dreams don't always come true as I discovered a week ago when I found out she was engaged to Owen.

Owen Price is the biggest jerk I know. For one thing, his reputation as a player is known championship-wide. He once boasted about sleeping with over one hundred girls in one season. I know without a doubt he's cheating on Vivi.

So, the thought of her with that man almost drove me insane that night. But my mum's counsel and prayers made me see it all in context.

The night is darkest before dawn.

The pain I feel every time I picture her with him shall pass. It is just one more thing to endure.

And with that clarity, I set my focus on working with my team to get through the playoffs. It seems that finally, the coaching has worked, and we have a winning team. Because this afternoon, we were fire on. Sure, it took us the first half to get our rhythm. But we were unstoppable in the second half. We still have a return match at Longmead Athletics. But I'm confident we're going to Wembley for the Playoff Final.

So, it's been a very good day.

And then to top it off, when we got back to the locker room and after I showered and was changing, I check my phone and saw a message from Vivi.

*Good luck with today's match.*

She'd sent me a message. And like that, I was thinking about her again, even though I'd promised myself I wouldn't.

Don't get me wrong, it's not like I haven't been with many women.

For a professional athlete, playing off the field is like a rite of passage. I've been with more than my fair share of women. Orgies, I've had them.

When you're a young footballer, away from home and those who anchor you, there's always risks and temptations. When you start earning the big money, those temptations quadruple. You end up with more money than sense. You want to experience the world and everything in it.

So, I'm no angel. I've lived a reckless, debauched life. But it all got old very quickly, and I walked away from the fast life.

Then I met Vivi and knew I wanted a future with her, to have a family and build a life together.

Yet, it seemed she'd chosen a different man to do those things.

So, when I got her text this evening, I don't think I've ever called anyone so fast before.

Hearing her voice transported me back to Zanzibar and the glorious twenty-four hours I spent with her.

Before I knew it, I forgot all the reasons I shouldn't be talking to her, and now, I'm driving over to her place.

Of course, I'm going there because I'm worried about her. The things she said about Owen got my hackles up. Owen has a mean streak a mile wide, and I have no doubt he would mete out punishment on Vivi if he felt slighted. Her talking about leaving him was good but dangerous. I can't trust the man not to hurt her.

When I arrive on her street, there isn't a parking spot outside her house. There are parked cars on both sides of the road because the residences don't have driveways. So, I drive a few metres down and park on a side road. The streetlights are on, but the area is dark and quiet. This is the suburbs, and most of the lights in the Victorian-style houses are off. I walk back down the pavement and climb the stairs to the main entrance. Then I pull out my phone and call her. She answers straight away.

"I'm at the door," I say and press the bell for her apartment. There are three listed on the panel.

"Come in." She buzzes me through the main entrance.

As I walk in, a silver sports car reverses out of a parking spot across the street and then speeds past very loudly. I don't see the driver, but I shake my head at how anyone could be so inconsiderate to their neighbours at this hour.

I make sure the main door clicks shut behind me. Shared entrances can be a cause of security failures. The foyer is well lit, and there are stairs going up to the next floor. The door at the end of the corridor creaks open, and Vivi's head pokes out.

"Hi, Asher," she says. "Come in."

"Hi." I walk down the corridor and into her flat, shutting the door. She flicks the lock in place.

And I'm hit by how beautiful she is. I've tried not to think about her all week. Have pushed her out of my mind. But standing in front of her, it hits me again.

Her hair is covered in a scarf, and she's wearing purple PJs that match. She looks cute and sexy at the same time.

Her face is clean and makeup-free. Her eyes have flecks of gold and amber over the bronze, and they hold me captive, keep me breathless.

Her lips are wide and luscious. Lord, forgive me, but I want to taste her, plunge myself into her and discover how sweet she is, even though I know she still belongs to another man.

With that in mind, I search her hand, looking for the jewellery, the symbol of her commitment to Owen, and I don't find it. Her hands are bare.

My heart races, and I step towards her. "The ring. You're not wearing it. Did you take it off because I was coming over?"

She lowers her gaze and bites her bottom lip.

"I took it off because I'm not with Owen anymore. Not in here." She places her hand on her chest over her left breast. "I haven't been with him in my heart since Zanzibar, since you."

She looks up at me, and I fall into her mesmerising eyes as her words register. Is there a possibility she wants me? I know what she said on the phone earlier about breaking off her engagement to Owen. It's one thing to end her last relationship and another to want one with me.

"Are you saying you want me?" My voice is a husky whisper as I bend over her. I cup her face with both hands, tracing my thumbs on her silky cheeks.

"Yes," she whispers back, her long, thick dark lashes fluttering.

Her word is like the flick of a lit matchstick at a kerosene-soaked firewood. Just a brush— *voom*—and the fire spreads down my body, consuming all my inhibitions, my principles and patience.

I slide one hand to the back of her neck, and a needy moan escapes her. I tip her head up and dip mine until our mouths are only inches apart and her ragged breath feathers my face.

"Lord knows I should have kissed you the night we met, while we lay under the stars," I speak in a low voice and our breaths mingle.

There's a shimmer in her eyes as her voice catches. "You should have."

Digging into the little restraint left in me, I groan at her words and close my eyes briefly. I would rather savour her than rush through it all like a savage. It's our first time, my first time tasting her, and I will not be the reckless, selfish boy chasing pleasures.

I trace the bow of her lips with my tongue. My right hand travels down her back and cups the swell of her butt through the satin trousers. I bring her body into mine, and we're touching from chest to legs. She must feel the press of my enlarged dick against her belly. I can't hide it any more than I can hide the way she makes me feel.

Her hands slide up my arms and across my chest towards my shoulders as I capture the fullness of her bottom lip and suck vigorously. She closes her eyes and makes a moaning sound in her throat as she presses into me. Then her fingers are on my nape, and she's on tiptoes, holding onto me.

I cup her butt with both hands and lift her up so we're both at eye-level. Then I back her up against the wall, and she wraps her legs around my hips.

"Tell me what you want," I rasp against her mouth.

The things I want to do to her. But I can't because I need to know she's with me every step. I need to know she's choosing to be with me even while Owen's shadow hovers over us.

She wriggles against me, leaning in, mouth open. She nibbles my bottom lip, and I swear it goes straight to my dick. I want to dive right into her, but I also want her to set the pace.

"Asher," she moans as I flick my tongue against hers. "Kiss me like you mean it."

The last of my self-control dissolves with those words. I've tried to be a gentleman, tried to do the decent thing. Right now, all I am is a desperate man, desperate for the passion this woman can show me, desperate for the sensations she will evoke in me.

Using the anchor of the wall to keep us upright, I grip her head with one hand and waste no time diving into her mouth with my tongue, kissing her like a dying man. Our tongues tangle and tango, suck and slide against each other. Our teeth bite and beg for more. I taste her like I've never tasted anyone else. It's the best first kiss I've ever had.

We come up for air, and I turn my attention to other delicate parts. Her cheek, neck, collar, making love to every exposed part of her satiny skin that I can reach with the lick of my tongue, brush of my lips, and the tug of my teeth.

"Asher ... please ... Asher," she whimpers, wriggling and writhing against me.

"Do you want more?" I will do anything she desires. I've been hers from that first moment we met in Zanzibar.

"Yes, more. Please," she pleads in a rushed, breathy voice.

She can command me, and I'll obey. But I love that she's pleading. It's my undoing. I came here to keep her safe. To protect her. I didn't mean to touch her. Didn't mean to kiss her. Now, I'll do whatever she wants.

I will fall into temptation and probably burn for it.

"Show me where you need me." My voice is so raspy, I can barely recognise it.

She lowers her hand and cups her left breast through the night shirt.

I reach down and undo the buttons, and I let the lapels fall apart, revealing the plump boobs hidden there. The brown nipples are erect, taut. I cup the left fleshy breast and squeeze gently.

She moans, head rolling back against the wall, eyes hooded as she watches me. I lower my head and lave my tongue around the nipple while she makes more glorious sounds of pleasure. Our eyes lock together, and I don't think I've experienced anything else so unbearably intimate. My chest squeezes tight. I take the whole nipple and suck it and more of her breast hard, and she keens, her body trembling.

"Oh god oh god oh god," she chants as I alternate from one breast to the other, giving each one plenty of my loving attention.

"I need you here, too." She places her palm over her lower belly near where our groins met through the fabric of clothes.

Her directness hardens my dick and penetrates my bones. She is making herself vulnerable and open to me. I can see it. It's a far cry from the woman in Zanzibar who erected impenetrable walls around herself.

Her mouth is open as I step back, and she lowers her legs to the wooden floor. She tugs the waistband of her PJs, and I halt her.

"Let me do it."

She traps the corner of her bottom lip with her teeth and nods.

Kneeling on the floor, I place my hands on her waistband, and my fingers graze her hip bones, making her gasp. I make sure my palm stays in contact with her skin as I push the satin trousers down, and she steps out of them.

I lean on her heel and look her over. Her spread legs are long, toned, and shapely in front of me. I follow them up, and she's wearing purple lace knickers which ride high on the hips but show off the dramatic roundness of her butt. Match them with the silhouette of the open night shirt showing off her luscious breasts and flat belly, and I have my own strip tease.

But my Vivi is a homegirl at heart, and the scarf on her head reminds me she was getting ready for bed, not a night club.

"Show me again where you need me." I'm kneeling in front of her, and I'm ready to worship her.

"Here." She covers her pussy lips with her palm through the knickers.

Nodding, I remove her hand and press her fingertips to my mouth while I raise my hand to their former position. "May I?"

"Yes," she replies quickly, breathily, and her stomach muscles clench as I graze my fingers over her knickers.

"You're perfect," I say as I lean forward and press my face to her skin, my tongue probing her belly button, and I graze kisses along the hem of the knickers. I tug it, and she wiggles her hips until it drops.

I lean back to admire her again. Her pussy is waxed, and as I trace my fingertip over the smooth labia, she trembles.

I knew I was into this woman before I came here today. But it's the way she responds to me that has my heart clutching and my body aching with the need to claim every part of her.

I caress the skin of her sensitive hips with my lips, brushing my tongue back and forth, tasting her. I've dreamt about doing this, and I can confirm it was worth the wait.

I part her labia with my fingers and dip my tongue between them.

"What are you doing?" she asks, her breath ragged and a little panicked.

"I'm licking your pussy." I look up, and her gaze darts away as if she's embarrassed. I'm not sure what the problem is. Is she shy about getting head? "Don't you like it?"

"It's not that." Her gaze darts around again before it settles on me. "I've never had it done before."

I jerk back. "*He* never gave you head?"

I don't say the name, but we both know who *he* is.

She shrugs. "I guess he doesn't like kneeling."

Okay. I change my rating for Owen Price. He's not just an asshole. He's a Grade A asshole.

Yet, a smile creeps onto my face because I can give her this first. "Then I would be honoured to be your first."

An answering smile blooms on her face, which makes me euphoric. She bends over and presses kisses to my temples. "Thank you."

Then she straightens, and I lean into her again. I run my nose along her pubic bone and breathe in the smell of her sex. It rivals any intoxicant. I want to stay high on her.

Her belly muscles ripple.

Then I part her labia and open her to my gaze. She is wet and glistening, her clit swollen and flushed. I tug the clit between my lips, and a tremor passes from her toes to her head as she moans. I grab her left leg and lift it over my right shoulder. This opens her up even more and spreads her out. I get to feeding again, lapping her, sucking her while gripping her butt with one hand to keep her steady. I'm like a man who has been starved and I'm at an all you can eat buffet.

She rocks her hips, pushing her pussy into my face, her fingers holding my scalp as if she doesn't want me to get away.

I don't want to be anywhere else but right here, worshiping this woman like an acolyte the way she deserves.

"Asher ... Asher." She sings my name constantly, and I know she isn't far off when I look up.

I suck and lick harder until her body bows, her leg tightens around my shoulder, and her hand digs into my scalp.

"Ye—es," she shouts, her expression wondrous and suspended in ecstasy, and she stays like that for a few seconds before she comes down, her eyelids heavy-lidded.

I scoop her into her arms, and she clings to my neck as I walk down the corridor and into the bedroom with the open door.

# 15

## Vivi

The dream is vivid, and Asher is with me. We're sleeping under the stars with the sound of the sea waves in the background. I'm nestled into his warm embrace, and his strong arms are around me.

I know this dream because I lived it, spent a wonderful night with him. He offered me himself and the world on a platter.

But this dream is distorted, different. We have company. Someone is standing at the foot of the bed. He's in the shadows, watching us, and I can't see his face. He holds a small object in his hand, something that catches the light.

I jerk upright, awake, my PJs sticking to my sweating body as I shiver. My gaze darts across the space. It's daylight, but the patter of rain hits the window behind the drawn curtains. I'm in my bedroom, on my bed. Asher is beside me.

He's awake and sits up, too. His voice is groggy. "What's the matter?"

"Nothing." I flop on the bed, wanting to shake off the nightmare which has been plaguing me for days.

He leans on his elbow and turns on his side to look at me, his brows furrowed. "Tell me, please."

He removed his shirt, jacket, and shoes last night and is wearing his white vest and trousers in bed. They're a barrier, signifying a line he's not willing to cross. Yet, I hope. Although he caressed and kissed my body last night, eliciting the most glorious orgasm I've ever experienced, he didn't penetrate me. Not even with his fingers. He's determined to retain some self-control and respect. I value his integrity.

Last night, I could see the hope and passion in his gaze when he noticed I wasn't wearing Owen's ring. Then when I told him I wanted him, it was like I released him from bondage. The rest was inevitable. Even though it was forbidden, I wanted him as much as he wanted me. We both crossed that line willingly. I have no regrets.

However, I need to be careful. *We* need to be careful. His concerns about Owen are not unfounded. While my soon-to-be ex-fiancé hasn't done anything violent yet, I can't discount it totally.

Now, it's the worry in Asher's voice which unravels me. I can't keep secrets from him. He's providing a safe space for me to be me. He shares himself with me freely. I need to learn to share myself with him equally.

Staring at the white ceiling, I bite my lip. "It's just a nightmare. I've been having similar ones for the past week."

"Can you describe it?"

He's stroking my arm up and down gently, soothing me.

"It's like at first I'm dreaming about the two of us on the hammock bed, but along the line, someone else intrudes in the dream, and I wake up feeling as if someone was in the room with me.

Obviously, I think it's all part of the dream because there's no one else here but the two of us. My mind is playing tricks on me."

"Hmmm," he murmurs, his forehead rumpling deeper.

"What is it?" I ask as I can see his mind working.

"I think it's more like your mind warning you about something. Do you mind if I say a prayer for us?"

That catches me off-guard. I know he's a Christian. He doesn't hide it. His actions except for last night are proof of his faith. But I didn't know he was that kind of Christian. On the other hand, no one has ever prayed for me personally. There are the prayers in church when I attend. When I was little, I listened to my mother pray.

"You want to pray for us?" I don't object to his prayers. It's the 'us' that has me curious.

"Yes, us." He sits up, his back to the headboard, and I sit up, too, matching his posture. "You do realise that last night changed things between us. I'm no longer on the outside of your life looking in. I'm in your life. We did something I promised I wouldn't do with any woman again except my wife."

"I don't understand."

He takes my hand. "When I gave my life to Christ, I promised I wouldn't have sex again except with the woman I married."

"Oh my god. You've been celibate?"

"Yes, for five years. Until last night."

I know what that means, and I'm filled with mortification. "I made you fall into temptation. I caused you to sin. I'm sorry."

"The only person responsible for my actions last night is me." He sounds outraged. "I made the choice to make love to you. My choice. I hate the concept that women cause men to sin. God gave every one of us willpower. How we choose to use it is on us as individuals. So please don't say that again. You didn't cause me anything. In any case, we have all sinned and fallen short of His Glory. If we repent, we shall be forgiven. That's His Promise."

He is as understanding as ever, and tears well in my eyes. He pulls me into his arms and presses his lips to my temple.

"Shall we pray?" he ask.

I nod and whisper "yes" as my throat clogs up.

We climb down and kneel beside the bed. He holds my hand and starts praying. It isn't long or show-off like some people in church. He offers praise, asks for forgiveness for our sins. He requests for the spirit of discernment so we can make the right choices and the strength to overcome our troubles. He prays for our safekeeping and for our family and friends, too. Afterwards, we chorus "Amen."

He helps me rise, and we sit on the edge of the bed. I don't know if it's the prayer or his presence, but surprisingly, I feel at peace. I know there's trouble coming, but I'm not scared like I've been for months.

"What do you have planned for the day?" he asks, still holding my hand.

"I have an article to finish, a couple of submissions to make, and I need to call my agent," I reply.

"Your agent. You have a booking agent?"

"Yes. I've done some modelling, and I do some brand partnerships for social media."

He grins. "Yes, I've seen your social media pages. You're doing well."

"Thank you." I tug at my night shirt, taking this as a cue to tell him about the TV show. "I wanted to ask you, would you ever consider doing a TV show?"

He tilts his head in contemplation. "I won't mind presenting or discussing football on TV."

"Would you consider a reality show?"

He frowns. "Like a documentary?"

"Like *Love Island*."

"No."

"Oh." My face falls. I could have guessed he wouldn't want to put his private life on display.

His frown deepens. "Are you doing *Love Island*?"

"No. But I've been invited to do a new reality show for a streaming service. It's for couples?"

"Couples?"

"Yes. That's why I accepted Owen's proposal. My agent, Emily, thought the two of us would be great on TV."

"Oh." He stands and moves away from me, and I miss his touch, his warmth. "But you said you were breaking up with Owen."

"I am. That's why I want to speak to Emily today. I want to let her know that I won't be with Owen."

"But won't that disqualify you?"

"It will unless I put someone else in his place." I meet his gaze, and his eyes widen.

"You want me to take his place on the show? No, I can't, Vivi. That's not me. If it was a sports show, I might consider it. But anything that involves egos and manipulations and popularity contests, count me out."

When he puts it like that, I can see why it might not be a good idea, and I don't want to do anything else that would cause him to fall into temptation. I know what he said about last night not being my fault, and I love that he defended me and women the world over. I still don't want to do anything to make him stumble.

"Okay. I'll call my agent and tell her I'm pulling out," I say, decision made.

"Oh, Vivi. I'm sorry." He returns to my side.

"No. There will be other opportunities, I'm sure. You said it yourself. We're in this together. We have to watch out for each other and ensure we don't cause the other to falter."

"Thank you. Okay. I haven't got much to do today. Coach gave us the day off following yesterday's win. So, I can hang with you for a bit, if you don't mind."

"Of course. I work from home except for when we record the podcasts or when I have physical meetings."

"Good. I'm going to order breakfast on the app. Do you want anything in particular?"

This man keeps surprising me. He didn't ask me to cook breakfast like someone I know did. I tell him what I want, and while he orders, I go in the shower. When I come out, he says he has to get his gym bag from the car because it has his toiletries and a change of clothes. He pops downstairs, and when he buzzes the main door, I let him in. I dress while he's in the shower. He's out and still putting his clothes on when the food arrives.

Afterwards, we sit at the small dining table and eat breakfast. He connects his phone to my Bluetooth speaker, and the playlist is wonderful— a mix of gospel, UK rap, and RnB. I know most of the songs. When 'Blinded by Your Grace' by Stormzy starts playing, we both sing along. We laugh and tease each other. We even get up and dance to the 'Big God' song by Tim Godfrey. We're relaxed and seemingly in tune with each other, and I love it. I didn't think I'd ever be this carefree in a relationship. This is a far cry from what I experienced with Owen.

Of course, it means I don't get to do any work until close to midday. But I do call Emily and tell her I'm withdrawing from the reality show. She's disappointed but accepts my explanation. However, she warns me Owen's agent won't be happy because they were keen to sign the deal. I tell her it's no longer my problem.

I get a message from Temi when she lands at the airport. Uncle Segun is picking her up and bringing her home. Asher decides it's his cue to leave. He wants to give me space and time to talk to my bestie and explain the situation, which makes sense.

I'm sad to see him go, but it's for the best. I walk him to the main entrance, and he kisses me on the cheek. We haven't had any mouth-to-mouth contact since last night, and I miss it.

I stand at the open door and watch him walk down the stairs. At the bottom, he turns and waves at me.

"Asher Uzodimma!" someone calls out.

He turns as two people run across the street. One's holding a camera, the other a microphone. Shit! Reporters. What are they doing here?

"Is it true that you're having an affair with Owen Price's fiancée?" one asks.

My belly turns over, and I'm frozen to the spot as Asher tugs the hood of his sweatshirt up and hurries down the pavement, avoiding them. The camera operator turns in my direction, and I quickly slam the door and race to my apartment, my heart racing. Body trembling, I shut the door and slip to the hard floor.

What the hell just happened out there?

# 16

## Asher

The night is darkest before dawn.

The proverb is on replay in my mind because I seem to have fallen into a pit, and there is no light at the end of it.

I've had a nightmare week which started as I was leaving Vivi's house. I was accosted by reporters with flashing cameras and microphone shoved in my face.

"Is it true that you're having an affair with Owen Price's fiancée?"

The next morning, torrid headlines were splashed across the tabloids.

**Goalpost Betrayal: Star Striker's Love Match Ends in Offside Affair!**

**Red Card Romance: Football Ace's Wedding Plans Tackled by Scandalous Side-line Affair!**

It's been horrendous, especially since 'sources' close to Owen Price claim the affair has been going on for months. I have no doubt the 'sources' is the asshole Owen himself.

I don't see Vivi again for the rest of the week. But I call her every night. She's distressed about the headlines, understandably. But we talk and share a quick prayer before bed, and it gets us through until the next night. Thankfully, her flatmate Temi is back so she's not alone.

Of course, it meant that by the time I arrived for training on Tuesday, my so-called affair with Vivi was the topic of contention amongst my teammates rather than our upcoming return-leg semifinal match against Longmead Athletics. Most of them could barely look me in the eyes while we trained.

Of course, this translates into our game on Friday. The first half is abysmal, and we are losing by one-nil because none of the team will pass to me or they fumble my passes.

During half time, coach gives all of us a good talking to. I honestly thought he would bench me. But he plays me in the second half, and when a free kick gives me possession of the ball, I head to the goal line, dribbling everyone in my path. When I see the opening, I shoot without hesitation, and it flies over the goalkeeper's reaching hands into the net.

Goal! The celebration is muted, and only a few of my teammates congratulate me. I don't mind. It's more important to me that we didn't lose than getting accolades at this point. When the final whistle blows, I'm just grateful we've made it into the Playoff Final at Wembley next week. It's a draw, but we're through thanks to our previous win.

After the match, the tension is still high in the dressing room.

"What is it with some people stealing from other people?" James Morrison comments.

He's a forward and our captain. He thinks I should have passed the ball to him instead of scoring. Well, I passed the ball to him through the game, and he didn't score. So, I don't care if his feelings are hurt.

"Or stealing other people's girlfriends," Ricardo Ramos adds snidely, and everyone laughs.

"Well, if people treated their girlfriends with respect, they wouldn't have to worry about other people stealing their women," I snap.

I've had it with silently tolerating their shit for the past week. Yes, I messed up, but which one of them hasn't.

James shoves me against the wall. "You're despicable."

"Don't fucking touch me." I shove him back, and we nearly get into a tussle.

"Guys, hold up." Xander Mitchell, a defender, steps in and pulls James back.

"Ash, come on." Nonso Chijuka, a midfielder, tugs me, too, separating us.

I allow him to drag me away only because he and Xander were the ones who congratulated me for the goal earlier. They have my back, and I respect it.

"Black," I use Nonso's nickname, shrugging him off, my anger still brewing. "I've been on this team for three years, and most of you know me personally. You know me. And yet, you read a newspaper headline, and you all condemn me as a cheater. Not one of you has asked me if it's true or not. I thought you know better than to believe everything you read."

After my speech, I slump on a bench and start packing up my things into the gym bag.

Silence falls on the locker room as everyone goes back to their kits and getting changed.

"He's right," Xander speaks up. "We all know Owen Price is an asshole on and off the pitch. Are we really going to take his word without question?"

"And he's in a rival team we're playing next Sunday in the Playoff final. Do we want to let him into our heads so that Duke Park Rangers—" Nonso spits "—defeats us even before we turn up for the match? I don't know about the rest of you, but I'm here to win titles."

"So am I," Tray Ellis says.

"And me," the rest of the team choruses.

The mood in the dressing room improves although James Morrison is still glaring at me. But I don't care. I'm glad to have some if not most back on board.

\*\*\*

The next day, I show up to the youth centre attached to my dad's church. I volunteer as a youth leader and a sports coach, and most of my work here is done post-season.

However, as I walk in, I'm pulled into the office of the senior coach who tells me I've been suspended as a youth leader and I won't be allowed to interact with the youth members. He tells me to go talk to Daddy GO.

I get into the car and drive to my parents'. I'm ready to rip into someone because I didn't expect to have the rug pulled out from under me like this.

I stomp past my sister who opens the door and greets me with a murmur, and head towards his private den. It's a Saturday, but I bet he's doing consultations. I'm correct because when I push the door without knocking, my dad is behind the desk, and there's a man in the seat on the other side. His assistant.

"Asher, not now. I'm in a meeting." He dismisses me without a second glance.

It only winds me up more. I'm tired of being dismissed and ignored as if I don't matter. "No, Dad. I'm not leaving until you hear me out."

He looks up and glares at me, but I don't budge. I'm not a child anymore, and he needs to recognise it.

"Please excuse us," he says to the man who gets up and walks out.

As soon as the door shuts, I move towards the desk. "You suspended me from the youth leadership team without telling me."

Dad tilts his head. "I'm sure Deacon Jones told you."

"That's not the point. Why am I suspended?"

"Do I need to spell it out to you? We cannot have you leading young people with the character you display. We can't have you setting the wrong example."

"I'm your son. When are you going to start giving me a break?"

"Actions have consequences!"

"So, I must be punished for falling in love?"

"Falling in love? Is that what you call it these days?"

"I don't deserve your scorn. Dad. I work hard. I help those kids."

"Now, someone else will help them. You're not the only talented athlete in our congregation."

"I'm your son!"

"And you think that entitles you to misbehave? You need to check your arrogance—"

The door swings open, and my mother walks in, preventing me from replying, which is as well. I don't think my father would like my response.

"Asher, I didn't know you were here." She looks from me to my dad as she steps up and gives me a hug. "I heard loud voices."

"Dad kicked me off the youth leadership team," I reply.

She glances at her husband and back at me, as if this is news to her.

"I'm sure it's just for a little while until things settle down," she says in a calm tone.

But I can read between the lines. Dad didn't tell her either.

"I only found out today from Deacon Jones," I gripe.

"He's in charge of the youth leadership team. It's his job to tell you." Dad sounds annoyed.

"I didn't even get a hearing. Didn't get to defend myself."

"Did you or did you not have an affair with that girl?"

"Her name is Vivian Osondu, and she is going to be my wife."

My mum gives a small smile.

My dad gasps. "You can't be serious. You are the bishop's son, and she is of the world."

"So am I. And if I'm your son, you will welcome her to this family." I turn and press a kiss to Mum's cheek. "I've got to go, Mum. Don't forget your tickets for Sunday's game will be sent to you via courier."

"I'm looking forward to it." She smiles and hugs me tight. "And I look forward to seeing Vivi again. She will be there, right?"

"Of course, Mum. See you on Sunday."

## 17

## Vivi

This must be my week in Hell because once the shit hits the fan, it doesn't let up.

I was there when reporters showed up at my doorstep as Asher was leaving my building on Monday afternoon.

I had to send Temi a message to warn her reporters are outside our flat so she doesn't get ambushed by them. When she eventually got in with Uncle Segun, I had to explain what happened with Asher.

She immediately thinks it is Owen's doing. But I can't figure out how he knew Asher was here. I call Owen, but he doesn't answer my calls.

When Tuesday arrives with the terrible headlines across newspapers and online articles, she is proven right. They claim Owen's sources told them the affair has been ongoing for months.

I'm filled with outrage, and he doesn't answer when I call him. I leave him a scathing voice note telling him our relationship has been over since February. I tell him to go to Hell with his lies.

Asher advises me to change the locks to our entrance doors. He thinks Owen has a set of keys to my flat. I never gave them to him. But now I know how vindictive he is, I don't doubt this aspect. I discuss it with Temi, and we book the locksmith who changes the locks on our entrance door. We talk to the landlord about changing the locks to the communal entrance, and he says we have to pay for it. Asher says he will cover the cost, but I don't let him. Temi and I share the costs. The other tenant we share an entrance with agrees for us to install a smart doorbell with video camera to record everyone who uses the communal entrance. I feel safer with the new security.

On Wednesday, my agent calls and says she won't be able to get me any gigs for the near future. Women always come out the worst in scandals and lose out on deals. I thank her for her honesty. She tells me she has been contacted by news outlets who want to interview me and hear my own side of the story. I tell her I will think about it. I don't want to feed the trolls while Asher still has the playoffs to get through.

On Thursday night, I sit on my sofa with Temi and watch Duke's Park Rangers play Eastborough Rovers on home ground in Chapel Road Stadium. It's the second playoff semifinal match. For the first time since I met Owen, I'm supporting the other team. I boo each time he has possession of the ball and cheer when the other team scores. Unfortunately, DPR wins the match by two goals to one. They are in the playoff finals.

And as long as Viva City Panthers don't lose their match tomorrow, DPR and VCP will face each other in the finals.

Excitement and anxiety course through me. It's a double-edged sword. I want the two rivals to play each other in the history-making final. However, I remember how Owen fouled and injured Asher months ago. I know my vindictive ex will try to do it again.

Later, Asher calls like he's done all week. He doesn't sound good. His teammates are giving him a hard time. I encourage him as much as I can and tell him our troubles will pass and we will triumph. I stay positive for him. He has his career at stake.

On Friday, we're back on the sofa, watching Longmead Athletics vs Viva City Panthers. The game is a shambles and ends in a one-one draw. It's obvious VCP has lost the cohesion they had in the earlier match.

Thankfully, they are in the finals and going to Wembley.

Actually, *we* are in the finals and going to Wembley. I have a new team, and when VCP takes on DPR next week, I will be cheering the Panthers. I am officially a Panther supporter. I don't care what anybody else says.

On Sunday, Temi and I share a cab to our parents'. It's the first time I've left the flat all week, and I'm glad to get out of those four walls. We go to church and sit in the back, trying to avoid prying eyes. It's not that I'm active in church. But my family are regulars because they've been attending the same church for years. When it's time for supplication, I pray for Asher, for safety and strength. I pray I will be a source of blessings to him rather than challenges.

After church, we hang out with our families. Before the football starts on telly, the women drag me into the lounge to talk about my breakup with Owen.

"Vivi, ada mmadu. You know we don't like to pry. But we have been hearing things," Auntie Dora starts. She is the younger of the twins and my second mother. She is the louder of the sisters, the inquisitive one. "The other day, Dele said you were trending on social media. But you haven't told us anything. Biko, what is really going on with you and that boy, Owen?"

"Mummy, Owen is a bad man," Temi speaks for me.

My mum says nothing.

"If you say he is a bad man, I believe you," Auntie Dora says. "I always thought he was arrogant. They way he behaved, like he was doing you a favour when I met him."

"Mummy, you knew he was arrogant, and you didn't say anything all this while." Temi frowns.

"Ha. Le kwa m. How can I say anything when the person wearing the shoes doesn't complain." She looks at me, implying I never complained about Owen. "If I had said anything, you would have said I was trying to kill your vibe, abi, how do you people say it these days."

She is correct. I probably wouldn't have listened if anyone tried to dissuade me from dating Owen two years ago. I worshiped the ground he walked on. He saw my naivety and took advantage of it.

"You're right. Owen deceived me. He deceived all of us into thinking he was a good person. But he isn't. He's put me through emotional torture, and if I'd stayed with him, I believe it would have escalated to physical. He's not happy I'm leaving him. That's why he concocted this story about me and Asher. This is his way of punishing me and Asher." My throat clogs up.

"Chai," Auntie Dora sympathises.

My mum gets up from where she's sitting and comes over. She sits beside me and hugs me. Tears wells in my eyes and fall. I've been through a gamut of emotions this week, but I haven't actually cried until now. There is something about a mother's embrace in times of distress than just opens up those wells and brings comfort.

Temi and Auntie Dora hug me in turns and hand me tissues.

"So, what is the deal with the Asher guy? Are you two dating?" Auntie Dora asks.

My cheeks heat, and I smile shyly. "After Owen rejected my proposal and I went to

Zanzibar, I met Asher in Zanzibar. He asked me out on a date, and I spent the most memorable twenty-four hours with him. He was charming and kind and respectful. I ended things with him before I came home because I wasn't ready to be in another relationship.

"When I came home, my agent offered me a place in a celebrity reality show. Then Owen proposed, and I thought maybe I could give Owen a second chance. Afterwards, things deteriorated, and he got increasingly abusive. I couldn't stand it anymore. I met Asher again at the end of season fundraiser at the Civic Centre, and I realised I still had feelings for him. I was going to wait until the playoffs was over to break off with Owen because I was trying to consider him. But then he told the press I was having an affair with Asher, and here we are."

"So how did Owen know about Asher?" my mum asks, frowning.

"I don't know. They met at the Civic Centre, so maybe he got jealous about Asher," I say.

"Hmmm. Vivi, I'm worried about your safety. You hear all kinds of stories about men who don't like it when women leave them. Please be careful. If you need to come home and stay here for a while, your room is available."

"Thanks, Mum. But I think I'll be alright. I have Temi, and we've changed the locks to the flat, and we have a door camera. So hopefully more secure."

"It is well," Auntie Dora says.

\* \* \*

On Monday, I call Dave to cancel our podcast recording session. I'm not ready to talk freely about anything. I'm too anxious about the upcoming playoff final. Also, Dave is a friend of Owen's, and I'm not sure where his loyalties lie in this debacle.

"Vivi, I know you're stressed, and I'm sorry that Owen is being such a dickhead. But there is something I need to show you. Can you come to the studio?"

"I don't know. I'm not going out at the moment because I'm worried about reporters." This business with Owen has made me suspicious of everyone. Maybe Dave told Owen about Asher. Then again, how would Dave know about Asher? I'm just confused.

"It's okay. I understand. Don't worry. I'll send it to you by courier."

"Okay."

Later, a courier arrives with a small parcel, and I sign for it. I take it inside and open it. It's a USB stick and a note scrawled by Dave.

*You need to listen to this. I'm sorry about what he's done.*

My hand is shaking as I open my laptop and plug in the USB stick. Then it starts playing. It's an audio from the podcast studio.

It starts off with me and Dave rounding off a podcast session. I remember the session. *Then the doorbell buzzes and the scuffle as I stand to answer the door. Owen walks into the studio. It's the day he proposed to me. The audio continues through the proposal and even after I walk out of the studio.*

"*Did you see that? The bitch just walked out on me. Who the fuck does she think she is. Telling me I'll think about it,*" *Owen yells.*

"*You need to calm down,*" *Dave says.*

"*Don't fucking tell me to calm down.*"

"*But I thought you didn't want to marry Vivi. Why are you proposing to her?*"

"*I don't want to marry her.*"

"*Then what is this about?*"

"*Let me show you something. You better not tell her about it or else.*"

"*Okay. What is it?*"

*There's silence for a few seconds.*

"*What is that?*" Dave asks.

"*She met him when she went on holiday,*" Owen replies.

"*Who is he?*"

"*It's Asher Yuzodeema. Panthers' No 11.*"

"*What? He wrote her a note? How did you get it?*"

"*How else? I saw it in her flat.*"

"*Mate, how did you see this in her flat when the two of you broke up.*"

"*Are you stupid or something? Of course I go to her flat when she's not there. I just want to know what she's doing since she blocked me from contacting her any other way.*"

"*Mate, Owen, listen. You don't want Vivi. Just leave her alone.*"

"*What? I should leave her for who? Asher fucking Church boy. Never. Now, mind your fucking business or else.*"

*There is stomping footsteps and a door slams and then silence.*

My heart is racing, and I slump into the chair.

Owen was in my flat without my knowledge. He must have had my keys. Asher and Temi were right all along.

Owen must have been coming here without my knowledge. Maybe even while I was sleeping alone while Temi was away. Maybe that's why I kept waking up feeling like there was someone else in the flat.

Thank God Asher suggested we change the locks. I haven't felt the presence in a week.

I feel sick, and I go to the bathroom and throw up. When I feel better, I call Temi and ask her to come home. I know Asher is in training, and I don't want to disturb him.

Temi comes home early, and she listens to the audio. She suggests we report it to the police, and I agree. We copy the recording, and she escorts me to the police station where I give them the USB device and make a statement. They say they will investigate, but I don't know if they will take it seriously. Cases of stalking and domestic abuse are notoriously under-investigated.

When I come home, I'm determined not to allow Owen to demean me and turn me into a woman afraid to live. I complete an online application for a restraining order against him. I also hire a lawyer.

I call Dave, and he apologises profusely. He didn't know what to do with the recording once I accepted Owen's proposal. I thank him for giving it to me.

I decide to not tell Asher about the audio evidence because I don't want him to lose focus for the match on Sunday. I will reveal everything to him afterwards.

The next day, I call my agent and tell her I'm willing to tell my side to the press, preferably a TV station. I inform her that I have evidence of domestic abuse. She says she will make enquiries and get back to me.

Hiding the recording from Asher is tough because we talk freely and I tell him everything else. I feel guilty when we chat, and I think he notices.

He couriers me VIP access to the playoff final. He says his family has a hospitality box, and I'm invited to join them in it. I have passes for four people, which means I can take Temi, Dele, and Uncle Segun.

My agent gets back to me. She got me interviews with different channels. With recent high-level profile cases of violence against women, DV is very topical at the moment. I select the ones I want to talk to, and she books the appointments. Because this is a developing issue, the schedules are for the next day. By the time the interviews are done, I'm wiped out.

On Sunday morning, the interview airs on Breakfast TV chat show. They play the full audio from the studio and bleep out the swear words.

Temi and I watch it as we eat breakfast. I upload the video that I have from when Owen proposed which is synced to the studio audio onto my page on YouTube. I share snippets across my social media accounts. All the posts go viral within a few hours.

Women are up in arms across the world, with people sharing their own stories of spousal abuse. And they are using Owen Price's name as a swear word.

Oh, I love being petty.

# 18

Playoff Final day is here, and I'm buzzed. It's a bright sunny day outside, and the light beams in through the partially open blinds.

I roll out of bed in the morning, kneel beside it, and say my prayer for the day. Then I stroll into my kitchen to get a drink of water while I check my phone. There are many messages.

From my mum: ***Asher, this is your day. No weapon fashioned against you shall prosper. Don't let anyone dim your shine. You are a winner. See you later, Mum xx.***

From my immediate older sister, Becca: ***Something to lift you up.*** With a link to a music app. When I click on it, 'Every Praise' by Hezekiah Walker starts playing.

My sister knows me too well. I listen to it as I check out the other messages.

Mak Phillips: ***You're taking home that trophy. See you at Wembley.***

Zafe Essien: ***Guy, no gree for anyone. You've got this.***

I chuckle as I read that. If no one else has my back, I know Mak and Zafe won't let me down. They didn't question my guilt about the so-called affair with Vivi. Once VCP booked a place to the playoff finals, they booked their tickets to be here for it. They've flown all the way in from Italy to be at Wembley today. They'll be watching the match live from the VIP hospitality box they've booked. I can't wait to see them later.

Then I read the text from Vivi:

*Hi Asher, I wanted to let you know that no matter what happens today, you are in my heart. I will be there cheering you on. Viva Asher! Viva Panthers! See you later* 😊 😊

Warmth fills my chest, and I'm grinning. Vivi will be at Wembley watching me play and supporting me and VCP. I know she used to support DPR, and I can imagine what it took for her to switch sides.

Just from her tone, I can guess she is in love with me.

*You are in my heart.*

Those words clarify it for me.

She loves me like I love her.

We haven't spoken those exact words to each other, but I believe it in my heart. She wants the best for me and I her.

Since I met her, I've tried to analyse why she is the woman for me. First, it was meeting her in the sports bar and realising her love for football. Of course, her beauty had a big part of it. Physically, she is my dream woman.

However, there were other aspects. She could have gone ahead and written the articles she'd wanted to write about my uncle's party and my footballing friends. But she didn't. I know she lost money from not posting any photos from her outing with us during the Stone Town tour.

Since we reconnected in the UK, she's shown consideration for me, especially for my faith. A lot of women are happy to hang out with me until they find out I'm devout with my faith and then they scamper. Even the women who share the same faith seem to only want me because I'm Bishop Uzodimma's son. They want the status that comes with being related to the man of God.

I spent twenty-four hours with Vivi the first time we met, and she didn't demand sex like many others have done in the past.

And when we did have the sexual encounter, I could see she was genuinely upset I'd broken my vow of chastity. Her subsequent commitment to making sure I stayed on the path of grace blew me away. I really wasn't sure how she would handle it, and I'm grateful for her.

Like I told my father, Vivi is going to be my wife, by God's grace.

With a smile on my face and Vivi on my mind, I return to the ensuite bathroom for a shower and a shave. My match day routine is established, and I don't deviate from it. I don't turn on the TV or radio or go online. Nothing must distract me from my focus.

I dress in my sweats and pack my gym bag. I eat breakfast and review match tactics on my tablet. There is an analysis of our opponent's playing manoeuvres and our strategy to break down their defences. I love the review of sports performance almost as much as I love playing the sport, which is why I'm thinking of going into coaching and management when my playing days come to an end.

Then I get into the vehicle and drive to the training grounds. My playlist is blasting from the speakers, putting me in the zone. It's the same playlist I use every match day. It's mostly UK rap and gospel. There's something about the energetic pulse of rap and the uplifting beat of gospel that sets me in the right mind to play football.

The pods are in my ears, and the music is thumping as I grab my gym bag from the boot of the car. Staring straight ahead, I'm in my zone as I head into the building. The past two weeks in the training grounds have been less than pleasant, and I don't need anyone killing my vibe.

However, the grounds staff are smiling at me, and one of them waves with a greeting. Not to be rude, I wave back. Perhaps they've decided I'm not a horrible person, after all.

I walk into the dressing room, and some of my teammates are already there. A few of them are huddled together, watching something on a device. They lift their heads, and I nod at them in greeting but don't stop. I walk to the bench under my locker and dump my bag.

I'm about to pull out a book from my bag when James Morrison shows up. He comes straight over to me, and I stand, muting my music, expecting a confrontation.

"Ash, can I talk to you for a minute?" he asks, his body posture relaxed.

"Yeah, what is it?" I reply, eyeing him.

"I want to apologise for my attitude over the past two weeks. I had no right to judge you based on someone else's accusations without getting your side of the story. I'm sorry." He hangs his head.

I don't know what brought this on, but I believe his apology is genuine. "Thank you, James. I accept your apology."

He smiles and extends his hand, and I take it in a firm shake. He pats my shoulder. "Don't worry. I'll make sure everyone is pulling together for the match. And we're going to keep that git Owen Price off your back."

I'm wonderfully surprised and impressed.

\*\*\*

Two hours later, we're stepping out of the team bus into Wembley stadium. It's amazing to be here after what has been an unpredictable roller-coaster season. Every footballer who plays in the English Football League looks forward to playing in this iconic stadium.

The team's energy is upbeat as we enter the dressing room. Some of the greatest players in the world have been in this dressing room. I take a moment to reflect and send up gratitude for this opportunity.

We listen to Coach's motivational speech, which ends with:

"In this arena, every pass is a duel, every goal a victory. We'll ride into this battle with our hearts fierce and our boots ready. This isn't just a game; it's the legend we'll leave on the field."

And we cheer loudly.

Not long after that, we're lining up and walking out onto the hallowed turf of the national stadium.

The atmosphere is electric. The crowd thunders. Light reflects off thousands of phone cameras. The stadium is more than half-full. It seems every regular supporter of the two teams in here. I notice the end with our prominent team colours showing banners saying, 'Go Panthers!'

I see a banner that reads 'KCT Youth Centre for VCP' and recognise the faces of the people holding the banners. KCT is Kingdom Come Tabernacle, my father's church. The kids from the youth centre are here. Adrenaline spikes through me. This has to be my mother's doing. She must have convinced my dad to allow the youth team to bring the group to Wembley. It's a great excursion for the kids who are fans of football.

And it's a great boost to me. I soak it all, letting the energy suffuse me as we go through our pre-match warmup.

The media has billed this match all week as a duel. A showdown between Owen and me. Between fierce football rivals. One headline referenced a famous old western movie:

**Showdown at the Goalpost Corral: Undaunted Panthers vs. Rampaging Rangers!**

It set the stage for an epic clash where honour, pride, and victory are at stake.

Honestly, I do feel as if my honour is at stake. If I were living in medieval Europe, I would challenge Owen to a duel to defend my name.

So today, I'm playing for me, my team, and my love, Vivi.

We stand still for the national anthem and then we have to shake hands with the opposition team. They stay in place while we walk past them, sticking out our hands for the shake. Although they shake my hand, most of them don't meet my gaze.

When I step up to Owen, he has a sneer on his face, and his eyes are wild. There's something off about him. For a man who was supposedly wronged by his fiancée and me, he doesn't quite look right. He looks deranged. I smirk because we call DPR 'Derangers' anyway. He doesn't shake my hand, and I step away after a few seconds.

The coin is tossed, and kick-off is explosive. In under five minutes, I score the opening goal, and the stadium roars in celebration.

Owen is more aggressive and blatant, and it seems to work at first when he scores for DPR ten minutes later. But we come back, and James Morrison scores. The spectators are like the twelfth man on our team. By half time, we're two goals to one up.

As I step onto the field after the break, I look up at the big screen, and the image halts me in my track. The camera is focused on Vivi and her cousin Temi. She's wearing the Viva City Panther's jersey I gifted her. My heart swells with pride because it's my shirt and has my name and number on the back. They are talking to each other and giggling. I can imagine Vivi's throaty laugh that hits me right in the chest with sweet, cosy warmth. They don't seem to know the camera is on them. She is so full of life and carefree. It seems all her troubles are forgotten. I want to capture the moment.

Then someone sitting next to them nudges Vivi, and she looks up at the screen. Her eyes widen in shock, but she recovers quickly. Smiling into the camera, she turns around, showing everybody looking whose shirt she's wearing. It makes me so ecstatic, and I'm high. I want to shout that's my woman, but she's saying it for me. The camera and the crowd love her.

And I love her so much.

One of my teammates shouts my name, and I realise everyone else is ready to kick off the second half. I run up to my spot and catch Owen's gaze on me. He appears furious. He must have seen me looking up at Vivi. I ignore him as the game restarts. He seems to totally ignore the ball and just runs at me, shoving me.

"Did you know I was her first." He sneers at me. "I've fucked her in every hole. So you're getting my leftovers."

My teammate calls the referee's attention, and after consultation with the lines person, Owen is given a yellow card. He seems ready to self-destruct, and I'm happy to facilitate it.

However, his words stay on my mind, and I have trouble getting back into the game. I can't seem to hit anything on target. DPR take advantage and equalise, making it two all.

I get possession of the ball again and start dribbling opponents. Then bam, pain rips through me as someone tackles me. I fly through the air and crash on the ground.

The medics run onto the field to attend to me. I grip my thigh, fearing it could be another debilitating injury. I lie in pain while they attend to me. From the corner of my eye, I can see the referee giving Owen a red ticket and sending him off.

The crowd chants a song, and I realise there is a Nigerian or African contingent in the crowd. I catch a line of the song:

*He no dey fall my hand. His always by my side. A very big God.*

I take it as a message, so when the medics want to stretcher me off, I tell them I want to play on. They spray something to numb the pain and give me a drink. Then they help me up, and I walk it off. When I run back onto the field, the crowd cheers.

I play on, and James Morrison scores again. Then I score, too. When the final whistle blows, we win by four goals to two.

It feels amazing, and I can barely control my joy.

Viva City Panthers are the Championship Playoff Winners.

The place explodes with celebration as we go around shaking hands with the DPR players. Thankfully, I don't encounter Owen again.

A microphone is thrust in my face as the reporters throw questions at me. I answer them as best I can. When someone asks about the recent allegations in the newspaper about an affair, I look straight into the camera and talk into the mike,

"All I can say is the love of my life is in the stadium today, and nothing will make me happier than to have her as my life partner. Vivi, please, will you be my wife?"

There is an uproar, and I step away from the mikes so my teammates can be interviewed.

Someone taps me on the shoulder, and I swivel.

Mum is standing there, dressed in a black and gold print dress, the VCP colours. She gives me a tight hug. "Congratulations. You did it. I knew you would."

Then she steps back, and I see her. Vivi. She is the most beautiful woman ever.

"Congratulations," she says as I wrap her up in my arms. "I heard your interview."

"And?" I step back to look at her face, and she's smiling.

"My answer is yes, I will marry you," she says.

I lift her up and in the air and shout, "She said yes!" into the nearest mike, and the crowd cheers.

It's a double victory. Viva City Panthers is going to the Premier League next season, and I got the girl.

# Bonus Chapter

## 19

## Vivi

Some things are unquantifiable.

The way I feel right now is one of them.

How can I quantify the boundless joy I feel or the ecstatic expression of Asher's face or body movement?

He proposed to me in front of fifty thousand spectators at Wembley. After he led his team to victory over Duke's Park Rangers in a thrilling football match.

Best proposal ever!

To top it off, Viva City Panthers are the Championship Playoff Winners and will play in the Premier League next season.

Fantastic!

So you can imagine the joy Asher feels. The joy I'm experiencing. There's nothing like this.

The crowd was amazing. It's like everyone has seen the interview I did or the viral social media posts. They cheered every time Asher had possession of the ball and booed at Owen. I could swear a section was chanting "Owen Price Abuser!" Or perhaps it was my imagination.

Asher seems oblivious to it all. Nothing can touch him, and he holds onto me as he hugs his mother again. I already greeted her when I saw her earlier. From her response, it seems she's forgiven me for the incident with Owen at the Civic Centre.

She is super excited for him, just like I am. He holds onto her with respect and love. I can see he adores her and I'm reminded of the first time I met her a month ago. The two of them have mutual respect and love for each other. I admire it. A man who respects his mother would respect his spouse, hopefully.

Not that I doubt Asher respects me. He's shown me respect from day one.

Then his coach taps him on the shoulder and I let him go, standing back.

"This is so amazing," Temi says loudly to be heard above the ruckus, giving me an excited hug.

"Congratulations!" Dele joins her in embracing me, reminding me I'm now engaged to Asher.

"Thank you." But I don't mind that my engagement to Asher has taken a back seat briefly. We'll fully celebrate it later.

This is Asher's moment, and I want him to bask in the glory. He has worked so hard to get here. His entire footballing career. But even more so in the past four months after he sustained an injury which kept him from playing for weeks.

Now he is celebrating with his teammates as they line up to receive the winners' medals. The place explodes with confetti, flashing cameras and roaring spectators. It is a historic moment. For the team. For Asher. For me.

Four months ago, I had a different boyfriend and a different team.

Now, I'm a full-blooded VCP supporter. Go Panthers!

I came here today to cheer my man on.

Asher Uzodimma is my man. The man who claimed my heart in an unexpected way.

Three months ago, I was heartbroken and seeking to escape my imploding life. I'd proposed to my ex-boyfriend, who rejected me spectacularly in front of hundreds of watching online followers.

In Zanzibar, I met Asher. I knew about him beforehand because he was Owen's rival on the field as a Viva City Panthers player. The rivalry between DPR and VCP has always been epic.

But I didn't know then he would battle with Owen for my heart.

He won it fair and square.

To be honest, I tried to find reasons Asher, and I couldn't be together. I didn't make it easy for him to claim my heart.

I tried to run, tried to hide, tried to rationalise.

I wasn't ready. Was not prepared to entertain another man after Owen.

Yet Asher came and demolished all my reservations. Tore my walls down.

In the end, I was left wondering what I was hiding, and why I was hiding.

Those twenty-four hours with him in Zanzibar still rank amongst my best days ever. Of course, the night he showed up at my apartment, worried about me because I told him I was breaking up with Owen, was ecstatic.

Owen, being Owen, tried to ruin everything by siccing reporters on Asher and accusing us of cheating. Meanwhile, he had no intentions of marrying me when he proposed.

Thank God for Dave, who gave me the audio recording of the aftermath of Owen's proposal. Evidence of his narcissism, his stalking behaviour. I made a statement to the police and filed for a restraining order against him.

But I didn't stop there.

I took it a step further. I granted interviews to two new channels, and they aired it this morning, while my social media campaign did the rest. Now the world knows that star footballer Owen Price is an abuser.

A niggle of unease ripples through me.

I'm worried.

Not about Owen. he can literally go to Hell.

I am worried about Asher. About how he'll take the news about my interview.

I didn't tell him about the audio recording Dave had given me. Nor did I mention I would do interviews with TV channels. I kept the information hidden from him for about a week.

The interviews aired this morning. I'm not sure if he's seen them or not. Knowing his match day routine, I doubt if he's been on social media or even watched any broadcasts today.

I want to talk to him first, before anyone else does.

"Vivi," Asher's mum comes up to me, beaming a smile. "Congratulations on your engagement."

She opens her arms and I step into them. "Thank you, Mrs Uzodimma."

Her embrace is soft and comforting.

"Mbanu, no," she says and I lean back, frowning, thinking I've done something wrong.

"I'm your future mother-in-law. The whole stadium witnessed it like our Umunna," she continues smiling and her tone holds humour. I'm not sure where she's going with this, but from my little Igbo knowledge, Umunna means kinsfolk. "So it only remains for you to sip champagne and give it to Asher, and your betrothal is complete."

"Mum, you're frightening her." A woman laughs as she steps up to me. "Don't mind my mother. If you leave it to her, you and Asher will be married tomorrow. By the way, I'm Becca, Asher's big sister."

Asher is the youngest child, so all his siblings are older. But he's told me about them and Becca is the immediate older sister. She is in her early thirties and is dressed in denim trousers and a black t-shirt. She is pretty and curvy, with her mother's face and similar features.

"It's nice to meet you, Becca." I hug her too.

"By the way, Mum is right." She leans back, still smiling. "I'm 'Sis', and she's 'Mum', to you from now on."

"Of course." I turn and introduce the people standing next to me. "These are my cousins Temi and Dele. And this is their father, Uncle Segun."

They do the rounds with hugging.

"We're all one big family now," Becca says.

"E remain small. We must chop the bride price," Uncle Segun says jokingly in Pidgin.

"That's for Mrs Osondu, a gift to her for raising the woman who captured my son's heart," Mrs Uzodimma says and holds my gaze. She is being witty, but she's also serious. The way she spoke says she holds my mother in high esteem. Asher probably already told her some of my family's history. So, she knows my mum is a widow. It's at times like this that I miss my father.

My throat clogs with emotions and tears smart my eyes. I embrace Asher's mum. "Thank you."

"You're welcome to my family," she says. "We'll take care of you."

I believe her promise and it fills me with warmth.

"Let's go back up to the hospitality suite," Becca says. "Asher will meet us there when they finish. He still has to do team photographs and other things."

I glance at where Asher is standing with his teammates, but he is engulfed in the crowd. Becca is right. We won't get to see much of him until the stadium empties and that won't happen soon.

So I follow the group back into the tunnel and then we take the lift to the hospitality level. The place is already busy. Press photographers approach us requesting to take photos.

"I am Asher Uzodimma's mother and this is his fiancée, Vivi," my future mother-in-law announces with pride. It's as if I'm the star prize and her son is lucky to have me.

Feeling weightless, I giggle as we pose for the cameras. I have no doubt this woman has my back. I've landed the Mother-in-law of the Year. She is not camera shy either. I suppose she is used to being photographed because of her son.

My respect for her also rises because she didn't pander to my uncle. I love my uncle but the idea of men collecting bride price for the women in their families rankles. I'm glad Asher's mother isn't toeing the same line.

However, I'm not sure if Asher's father feels the same way about women sometimes being sidelined in traditional marriage negotiations. Then again, Asher's father is a bishop. Does he condone traditional weddings?

"I was thinking," I say when the press people finally leave us alone. "Do you think it's a good idea to do a traditional wedding?"

"Of course it's a good idea," Asher's mum replies. "Unless you don't want one."

"No. I don't have a problem with it. But I thought because you ... Asher's dad." My cheeks heat because I can't seem to find the right words to express myself. I don't want to offend her. "I thought some Christians don't enjoy doing traditional weddings."

"There is nothing wrong with traditional weddings," she replies. "For it is written, 'Render unto Caesar that which is Caesar's and unto God that which is God's.' Matthew chapter 22 verse 21. So, if you're not opposed to it, then I would recommend the traditional ceremony as an introduction of the families, that is the in-laws. Then a church wedding to bless your union and welcome you into our wider church community."

Her explanation makes sense. "Yes, I agree."

"Good. I know you will need to discuss details with Asher. But we can probably schedule you in for a church wedding within six months."

"Six months? That seems soon," I reply without thinking.

"Well, you could wait for a year. But it means you'll both be abstaining for a year," she says casually as we walk towards where the rest of the group are gathered. They went ahead while the press mobbed us.

"Abstaining?" Her words click in my mind and my cheeks flame with embarrassment. "Oh."

Of course, I forgot Asher was celibate. I haven't been in the same physical location as him for two weeks. So, I haven't really thought much about sex with him. But now we're engaged. And his mother just implied we won't have sex until we get married.

I definitely cannot wait a year to make love with the man I love. If our one night of passion is anything to go by, I don't want to wait to share more sensual pleasures with him. Yet I don't want him doing something he swore he won't do until he gets married.

I guess we're going to get married soon then. At least we can become official once the traditional ceremony is done and we don't have to worry about booking a hall. We can have it at my mum's house. The church wedding can come as soon as there's a space on the calendar.

When I proposed to Owen, I didn't mind having a long engagement. Two-three years?

But with Asher I don't think I can wait six months, even.

I join everyone else at the table and servers bring drinks. I snag a flute of champagne. Then I realise I'm sitting next to Bishop Uzodimma's wife, who is drinking juice. Asher's sister is also drinking juice. Yet none of them comment about the alcohol in my hand. My respect for them grows. I'm not amongst judgemental people.

"Auntie," a male voice says.

I look up at the new arrivals and recognise their faces. Zafe Essien hugs Asher's mum first. He's with Mak Phillips. I'm surprised to see them here. The Italian Serie A football season ended earlier today. They must have flown out straight after their matches to be here now.

"Hi, Vivi," Mak says as I stand to embrace him. "I hear congratulations are in order."

"Thank you." I say.

He steps back and I see the females with them.

"You remember Ranti and Inna," he says.

"Of course. It's nice to see you all again," I reply.

"Same here." Ranti comes forward and embraces me. "Congratulations."

"Yes, congrats." Inna joins in the hug. "I'm sorry to hear what your ex did to you."

"Yes, me too," Ranti says. "He should be locked up."

"Thank you. The case is with the police, but I'm not sure what they will do. I'm just glad to have him out of my life," I reply, bile rising in my throat every time I recall the vile things that man did.

"And now women know to steer clear of him."

"Indeed."

"Anyway, onto better things." I quickly change the topic so the mood doesn't dampen. "Did you both fly into London just to be here today?"

"Actually, I'm on my way to Nigeria to see my parents. I booked the flight to stopover in London for today. I'm catching my connecting flight tomorrow."

"That's good. What about you, Ranti?"

"Me? I'm not that far away. I'm only a train ride away in East Anglia."

"You're in the UK? I didn't even know. We must get together. Can I have your contact details?"

"Of course."

We take a few minutes swapping numbers and following each other on the social media apps.

We're still chatting when Asher shows up. He's dressed in a smart casual navy suit with a white t-shirt underneath.

Butterflies flutter in my stomach as his gaze locks with mine and he makes a beeline for me. It's like no one else exists and I have to force myself to breathe when he stands in front of me.

"I heard what you did." He wraps me up in his powerful arms and heady spice. "You're amazing. I love you so much."

My heart races. It's the first time he's said the phrase to me. But... "You're not angry?"

I worried he'd be angry because I didn't tell him about the audio or my interviews beforehand.

"Of course not." He leans back. "I understand why you did what you did. You were trying to protect me, and I love you more for it."

Emotions choke me and I know I'm with the person I was meant to be with. "I love you so much."

He leans down and kisses me, and the world fades away.

Thank you for reading Against the Run of Play by Kiru Taye. Please leave a review on the site of purchase.

Do you want more of Asher and Vivi? Visit my website and sign up to my newsletter to be notified when about upcoming book releases including extended epilogues.

https://www.kirutaye.com/contact

For more books from the Viva City FC Universe, visit https://www.vivacityfcbooks.net/

**Viva City FC Season 1 Books:**
Game of Two Halves by Unoma Nwankwor
Against the Run of Play by Kiru Taye

# Other books by Kiru Taye

*The Essien Series*
Keeping Secrets
Making Scandal
Riding Rebel
Kola
A Very Essien Christmas
Freddie Entangled
Freddie Untangled

*Bound Series*
Bound to Fate
Bound to Ransom
Bound to Passion
Bound to Favor
Bound to Liberty

*The Challenge Series*
Valentine
Engaged
Worthy
Captive

*The Ben & Selina Trilogy*

Scars
Secrets
Scores

*Men of Valor Series*
His Treasure
His Strength
His Princess

*Enders Series*
Duke: Prince of Hearts
Xandra: Killer of Kings
Osagie: Bad Santa
Rough Diamond
Tough Alliance

*Royal House of Saene Series*
His Captive Princess
The Tainted Prince
The Future King
Saving Her Guard
Screwdriver

*Others*
Haunted
Outcast
Sacrifice

Black Soul
Scar's Redemption